KW-222-030

Deception

Eloise De Sousa

Copyright ©2013 Eloise De Sousa

All rights reserved.

ISBN: **978-1-291-54795-5**

No part of this book may be used or reproduced electronically or in print without permission, except in the case of brief quotations embodied in reviews.

This is a work of fiction. All references to real places, people or events are coincidental, and if not coincidental, are used fictitiously.

All trademarks, service marks, registered trademarks and registered service marks are the property of their respective owners and are used herein for identification purposes only.

EBooks are NOT transferable. Re-selling, sharing or giving eBooks is a copyright infringement.

6 9341 300070399

With thanks to my family and friends
for their love, support and patience
whilst I follow my dreams.

Amanda opened her eyes to a brilliant sunny day with the birds singing outside her window and a gentle breeze blowing the curtains in a seductive dance. She stretched out her arms and yawned, feeling the sleepiness shrug off her body and a lovely tug of hunger making her tummy rumble. Hmm, some breakfast and maybe a long, hot shower and wash her hair. She picked at strands of her long wavy brown curls and sniffed them. Definitely a shower! Her hair smelt like burnt cat. Not that she'd ever smelt a burnt cat but she imagined it couldn't smell much worse than her hair.

Suddenly, the curl withered in her hand and turned to ash, as did her other curls. She spotted her reflection in the mirror opposite the bed and watched as her hair disappeared in a puff of ash and smoke. She screamed as the rest of her head caught fire and watched in terror and fascination as the flames licked away at her bald scalp. Panic filled every pore and drowned out her shrieks whilst the fire swallowed her nightdress, engulfing her body. Heat tugged at her, pulling her body as though she was a rag doll.

"Mummy! Wake up! You're scaring me!" Tug. Tug. "Mummy please wake up. It's a bad dream Mum. Stop screaming please!"

CHAPTER ONE

PING!

The lift doors opened and I trudged my dripping carcass across the marble lobby to the glass doors, handsomely stencilled with Alann and Cook in gold. Maggie, the receptionist, gave me a cold stare as my coat made little puddles on the carpet, and she took in my bedraggled appearance with a raised eyebrow.

"Hi Maggie, my car broke down and I need to get dried before going into Jennifer's office. Have there been any calls for her yet?" I tried to put on my most professional tone but the sight of me must have put my voice out of sync with my appearance.

Unconsciously I straightened my back and my chin tilted up. She sniffed the air and looked down at her message board. I could tell she was not impressed at all. After a few seconds, she looked up with the same raised eyebrow and in a loud husky voice told me I had missed the call from China that Jennifer had been waiting for. I had the grace to blush and shuffled closer to the reception desk.

"Miss Glenson, please keep your dripping tentacles off my clean counter!" she growled, watching a little puddle form from my escaped lock of brown hair.

"I'm sorry," I said, trying to stifle a giggle at her ridiculously angry expression and my drenched condition. Monday had not started out the way I had planned it. But then again, Mondays never did!

Waking my five year old and trying to get out of the house in time for school and work required maximum effort, which I sometimes did not have on a Monday, and today was no different. Add to that a broken down car, pouring autumn rain and a precarious bus ride to work, Maggie's face expressed a distaste that I felt for being here standing in front of her and being judged.

I tried to hide my amused grin and glanced behind me to see if anyone else had heard her. A pair of coal black eyes that held a hint of amusement captured me in their intensity. Thick black hair was slicked back against a perfectly shaped dome and a golden brown complexion looked smooth over high cheekbones and a very straight nose. Thin lips turned into an insolent smile and one eyebrow was raised at my open assessment of his features. I could feel my cheeks heating up as a cold shiver tickled my spine. I quickly turned my attention back to Maggie and her scowl told me she had noticed my long stare at the client sitting in the visitor's chair. This did not go down well and if her eyebrow could have disappeared into her hairline, it would have.

"I will need you to get me the number so that I can call them back immediately. Thank you!" I said with a smile that I hoped expressed an apology.

She just harrumphed and answered an incoming call as though I was not there. With a sigh I turned and tried to make my way past the visitor's area with a bit of grace that I lacked earlier. My heart jumped when I saw the tall stranger stand up and walk towards me with purpose. His dark eyes held me in place and my legs refused move back out of the way.

A smile broke out across his handsome features, dispelling the grim expression that haunted his eyes. A deep crease on either side of his thin lips gave him a boyish handsomeness. His face told me that he had noticed my reaction to his approach and amusement twinkled in his laughing expression. I straightened up, unconsciously smoothing out my wet coat and hair with embarrassment lurching freely in my stomach which was suddenly full of butterflies.

"Excuse me, but you dropped this on your way to the Reception desk."

I looked down at what he held in his large hands. My soggy scarf hung limply from his fingers and I could see a drop of muddy water slowly plop onto his shiny black shoes. Stuttering, I tried to remember Jennifer's words about professionalism and showing the world a strong appearance, but my face and body seemed to revolt against me. My cheeks were hot and I tried to take the scarf without dripping any more dirty water on his immaculate appearance.

My fingers grazed past his and I gasped as an electric current surged through me. Looking up at him to see if he had felt anything, I could only see amusement growing with each passing second I behaved like a silly school girl. Straightening my shoulders again, I looked straight into his dark devilish eyes and said, "Thank you so much. Sorry about your shoes!"

He frowned and looked down to see what I meant about his shoes, and I took the opportunity to escape his gaze. I made my way past the blue covered executive chairs for visitors and out to the hallway leading to the various offices as fast as I could. My office sat at the end of the corridor and had a view of the sky and tree lined streets, busy with buses and cars down below. Without looking back I ran to my desk and put my bag onto the chair next to my desk.

The adjoining door to my office and Jennifer's opened before I had a chance to put my coat down or greet Emma who was placidly sitting reading her newspaper and sipping her steaming cup of coffee.

Jennifer entered the room with a frown on her face. She always looked like thunder on a Monday. I think she hated being called into the office at 9am when she usually managed to work from home until about 11am, and then worked from the office for a couple of hours before returning home to continue with her schedule late into the night. We had a messenger service that was kept busy sending documents back and forth to her loft apartment in a private residential building on the upper west side of Winnersh, a little market town close to Bracknell.

"You're late Mandy and that awful receptionist has had the audacity to place a call straight through to my office this morning. Where were you?" she said, her lips a thin line. Her skinny hands sat with displeasure on her narrow hips. Her long blonde hair cascaded down her back in a perfect pony tail and her polished brown knee-high boots shone under the fluorescent glare of the office lights.

"I do apologise Jennifer but my car broke down and transport was been held up this morning by the weather," I replied in my most professional voice. I could see her looking at my appearance and her lips compressed further.

Without turning her head to see Emma sitting up straight and booting up her computer as fast and as quietly as possible, she said, "Emma, get me China on the line and get a hot cup of coffee for Amanda. Bring it to my office please."

"Okay Jennifer!" was Em's quick reply as she picked up the receiver and dialled reception to get the number. She gave me a little wink and cheeky grin as she put on her posh voice to speak to Maggie.

"Amanda, please come into my office right now!" Jennifer called as she disappeared through the adjoining door to her office.

I quickly put my coat on top of my bag and tried to smooth down my hair into some semblance of order. Unfortunately I could feel the curls at my temples and knew that the rest of my hair would be full of waves and curls thanks to the soaking it received. Checking my pleated skirt and blouse to make sure it wasn't too wet and dishevelled, I stepped through to Jennifer's office. She had returned to her seat behind her desk and I could see the view of the River Loddon through the window behind her. The sky was clearing and little slivers of blue could be seen here and there. The sun was burning through the clouds and gave the river a peaceful hazy glow in the morning light.

"Sit down please Amanda," she said with a sternness that caught my attention and made me obey without a second thought.

"As I pointed out just now, Maggie put through a call this morning that should have been taken by you!" She raised her hand to stop my apology before it formed on my lips and continued. "That is not why I called you into my office. The message itself caused me concern and that is why I called you in here."

I felt myself move to the edge of the chair. What message could she have received to call me into her office? The severity of her face made it seem extremely serious. I was sure I had filed all the documents to the courts on time and mentally did a check list to make sure. Yes, everything was left in order on Friday. The only thing outstanding was this call to China, but that was just to speak to prospective clients that wanted representation in the UK once their business venture with a local company, Intercom, took off.

As if reading my mind, Jennifer said, "The call was not business related but a personal matter. Your personal matter."

"Is Zachary alright? Was it the school calling?" I asked thinking that they might have tried to call me on my way to work and I missed the call. Zachary was only five years old and everything I held important in this world. If it wasn't for him, I would not be in this country, freezing my ass off every day.

"No. No. Zachary is fine as far as I know. This is about your past Amanda." I didn't like the sound of that. The only past I had was thousands of miles away and on a different continent. No one knew where I was and I wanted it to stay that way. Five years was a long time to have disappeared, but I had a new life with my son and a lovely little home. Nothing was going to spoil my hard work to establish myself in this fantastic job as a legal secretary to the Senior Partner of Alann and Cook.

"It was a call about your mother and father." She stood up and came to sit next to me in the second visitor's chair. Carefully, she crossed her legs and looked directly at me as if to gauge my reactions. My shocked expression must have made her act out of character; she gently rubbed my shoulder. Jennifer didn't have a soft bone in her body and had worked in a male dominant environment to become Senior Partner, not through the advantage of her father owning half the law firm, but through her own hard work. I admired her for that.

The shock of hearing her mention my parents took my breath away. I had no family in this country and everyone back home didn't have a clue where I was since I ran away five years ago to escape retribution for a crime I had not committed. Add to that an unplanned pregnancy and being young and scared and you had me in a nutshell. I turned slightly to her wishing she would just spit out what she knew and end my agony. Nobody knew about my family back home or the circumstances of why I came to England. If they did, I would never have landed this job and would not have been able to support Zachary and have my lovely home.

"A lady by the name of Esther called. She said she is your grandmother and it has taken her nearly six months to trace you to this company. It was of vital importance that she reached you as there was a family emergency and she needed your help. She told me that she had some very sad news to tell you, and there is no easy way to say this Amanda. Your parents were involved in a car accident and were killed instantly. I am so sorry!"

Jennifer leaned forward and tried to hold my arm or hand. I didn't know. I couldn't focus on what she was doing. Her piercing blue eyes were watching me, and her grim expression showed her sympathy. She knew how important family was, as she worked side by side with her father and everyone could see the love and respect between them. How could this be possible? Mum and Dad were gone and I would never get a chance to apologise and say how sorry I was for their embarrassment. I had just run away and never looked back. My past had caught up with me.

CHAPTER TWO

"Are you okay Mandy?" Jennifer asked, her eyes taking in my expression. "I understand that you never spoke of your family and always assumed there was something there that you didn't want to discuss, but if you feel the need to talk, my door is always open."

"I have this lady, Esther's number, so that you can contact her and find out more details. She said she was not at liberty to discuss why she needed you so urgently, but I did promise her you would get in touch immediately."

I tried to open my mouth to reply but nothing came out. The shock of what she had said was slowly seeping through my cold wet body. Everything around me seemed to fall back and I could picture my parents as though I had seen them yesterday. My mother's disappointed, tear-stained face as she shook her head at me, and my father's anger showing in his green eyes. Always anger at something I did or said, never pleasing him enough. I didn't hear Emma come in with my coffee and didn't see her worried stare when she looked down to see if I was okay. It must have been strange to see Jennifer holding my hand and me staring into space!

The warm mug was placed in my hand and voices spoke behind me. Something about ordering a taxi to get me home and my work should be covered. An arm was placed around my shoulders and I was coaxed to drink my coffee while I waited. Waited for what? I looked around and saw Emma hugging me. Jennifer was back on the other side of the desk and speaking to someone on her phone. She gave me a tight smile of reassurance and kept talking. Emma squeezed my shoulder to get my attention back and told me to come with her to the other office. I got up without a fuss and walked through to our office where she sat me down at a small sofa near the window.

"Are you okay Mandy?" she said in a soft voice. Her normally cheeky expression or a twinkle in her eye was lost in a sea of worry over me. That was unacceptable. No-one needed to worry about me. I had to get a grip. I felt the need to reassure her and slowly tried to stuff my raw emotions inside so that I could focus again. I needed to focus. Looking down I realised I was still holding the coffee cup and slowly placed it on the little table in front of me.

"I .. I don't know Em" I replied, a croak sounding in my voice. "I just found out my parents were killed in a car accident and ... and ..." I couldn't say any more. The croak felt like it wanted to swallow my voice and I could feel tears pricking the backs of my eyes.

She rubbed my arm and said she was so sorry as I tried to concentrate on swallowing the lump in my throat and blink back the tears that threatened to come pouring out. I had to take control. There were things to consider.

Zoe for instance. Who would care for her now that my parents had died? I had always assumed my sister was safe in their company, away from my bad influence. What was I going to say to Esther? I had to get out of here and think.

Just then a call came through at Emma's desk and she quickly got up to take it. Without saying much, she put the phone back down.

"A taxi is here to take you home Mands. I can come with you to make sure you are okay and we can pick Zachary up from school on the way." She moved to get my coat and helped me put it on. I grabbed my bag and slung it over my shoulder. She was making her way to her desk to retrieve her coat from the hook behind her chair when I clicked back into action.

"No! Don't worry Em, please" I said hastily. "I will be fine and you need to cover for me so that Jennifer doesn't fall back on the work today."

She gave me a queer look that showed she was hurt by my refusal. I smiled and walked to her desk.

"Thank you, but there is nothing more we can do. If my parents died and it has taken them six months to find me, there is not much else to do, is there?" I could hear the coldness in my own voice and tried to smile to ease my harsh words, but I could feel Emma looking right through me, as though I were a transparent piece of glass. "I have to go home and sort things out. But thank you. I will call you tonight and tell you what has happened, okay?"

Emma nodded, but I could see from her expression that she was confused by my behaviour. I had to get out of here before anyone else had a chance to ask questions or offer help. Half running out the office and down the corridor, I never stopped to wave good-bye to Maggie but just ran through Reception to the glass doors and out into the lobby by the lifts. One glance to my right and I could see that the client I had embarrassed myself with had gone. Thank goodness the lifts were free and swiftly answered my call. I jumped into the closest one and it took me down to the ground floor where I ran out into the fresh autumn air and slowly warming day. The taxi was parked in front of the building and took me through the back roads towards Sunbury Lane where my home was located and where safety could keep me from questions I didn't want to face or answer.

After closing my door to the view of the retreating taxi, I made my way to my study at the back of the house. It wasn't really a study but an extra room Zachary and I used to chill out in, play with toys, or for me to do some work at the little desk I had stationed in the corner. I sat down on the swivel chair and stared at the notice board stuck on the wall in front of me. My parents were dead. Zoe was alone. Alone for six months, and it was my fault as I should have been there. Zoe had never done anything wrong to me and now she didn't have her big sister to look after her at such an awful time. The guilt overwhelmed me. Tears I had choked back in the office flooded over. Gasping for air, the sobs shook my body as I thought about my parents and my sister and all that I had missed these past years. I felt so alone. If only I could have stayed and fought for the truth. If only people had seen what had happened and not blamed me. I wouldn't have had to run away. Maybe Jason would be with me now and we could be a family with our beautiful son.

The thought made my head snap up and I wiped the tears away with an angry swipe at my face. No, Jason would not be with me because he had chosen Lola and they were married. There was no point in lying to myself about that. He never loved me enough to stand by me when the shit hit the fan and now I had to be strong. I could feel the tears slipping away and anger replacing them. I had to speak to Esther, my grandmother. I had to keep the darkness away and contain my anger. Now was not the time to lose it. There were things to be done.

Esther Munford was a stunningly beautiful woman who had aged with a grace that had many of her friends believing she had succumbed to plastic surgery. Her bubbly personality and sometimes whimsical outlook on life meant that she never took anything seriously enough to cause frown lines. Her greatest joy in life was becoming a grandmother. Life had been perfect and she was filled with a happiness that came from knowing her twighlight years would be spent with a purpose. She would not disappear like a wilting flower, hidden in the recesses of a stuffy nursing home.

Amanda and Zoe were two perfect little girls to dress up in pink and parade in front of the other grannies at her numerous tea parties. Maria, their mother, never seemed to mind and allowed their doting grandmother to take the girls on many adventures around town whilst she spent her time concentrating on helping her husband set up their family business and keeping it afloat. The Glensons had a printing company that had been built from scratch and, through word of mouth, the business was becoming one of the most successful in Harare. Having Esther look after the girls freed up their time to concentrate on deadlines and clients, and if the girls seemed a little wild at times, it didn't bother them too much. They had a vision of the strict Catholic private school sorting out their wayward behaviour and turning them into ladies when the time was right.

Alas, by the time Amanda reached her sixth year in school, they knew that they should have paid more attention to their daughter's upbringing. She was beautiful, tall and had an athletic, willow-like natural grace. With her stunning green eyes like her father's and waves of golden brown hair, every boy in the neighbourhood started sniffing her out like bloodhounds at a fox hunt. What an interest she had in all the attention she received from these young men! Amanda was spoiled by her grandmother and school was boring. Boys, on the other hand, loved to make her laugh, would fight over each other for her and made her feel as if she was a princess. Her easy smile and gentle ways made each boy's heart race and they wanted…no, they needed to look after her.

By the time she was in her second year of high school, she had gone through about five boyfriends, breaking their hearts whenever they wanted to get serious. Amanda might have been a flirt, but she was no fool. She knew how her parents felt about her having boyfriends at such a young age. Their disapproval over everything she did and with the strictness of Zimbabwean society, she kept her libido in check. More importantly, Amanda liked to flirt and have fun, but she also searched for the same love she had seen between her parents from a distance.

It felt as though they existed in their own personal heaven, and Zoe and her were just the products of consummation and not the link that made them whole. The girls craved their parents' attention and anger burnt deep inside at the subtle neglect. She knew that all these frivolous boys were just after a good time and were not old enough to be serious. She wanted to save herself for a man who would love her not just for her beauty but for what she held inside too. A burning desire to belong and be accounted for - not ignored.

Esther had watched over the years in despair at her son's lack of interest in his own daughters. She did everything she could to make them a family, but the business pulled him away, taking Maria with him and leaving the girls bereft of attention.

Realising things would never change, Esther confronted Maria and David. After a furious fight it was decided it was best to keep this wayward grandmother at a distance from their daughters. She was removed from the priority position and was only called upon in an emergency to look after the girls. Esther was saddened by the turn of events and decided to confront her son, pointing out the neglect that the girls felt at their parents' selfish ways. David was a tall, stubborn man who felt slighted by his mother's description of his parenting skills. He took exception to being criticized by the same woman who had never had the time to raise him properly because of her own frivolous nature. Instead of solving the problem and mending their relationship, all ties were broken and the family fell apart; Esther on the one side of town and David, Maria and the girls on the other. They never spoke for the next few years; until a terrible turn of events forced them together again.

"Hello, is that Esther Munford's house?" I asked, hoping and praying that the crackling telephone call to Zimbabwe would somehow cut off and give me an excuse to end the call.

"Yes it is. May I ask who is calling please?" said a voice in a thick Mashona accent. I could tell the voice on the other end of the line was probably my grandmother's domestic worker.

"Could you tell Esther that it is her granddaughter, Amanda, on the phone?" I replied, hoping Esther was out for the day.

"Hold on!" The phone was noisily put down and I could hear footsteps retreating and the same voice calling out. "Amai! Amai! There is a call for you."

"Who is it Kumbi? Who is on the phone?" another voice at a distance called back.

Kumbi shouted back, "She said she is your granddaughter!"

I could hear a woman squeal and the shuffling of footsteps grew louder as they approached the receiver.

"Hello? Amanda, is that you?" was a breathless question from a voice I had not heard in years. I felt my heart sink to my feet. How was I going to do this?

"Hi Ma, how are you?" What more could I say? The notice board in front of me just stared back at my wincing expression.

"Mandy, my darling, I'm so sorry!" I could hear the sadness in her voice and my tears welled up again. "Did your boss give you my message?"

"Yes, she did. Thanks!" I sniffed and looked around my desk for a tissue.

"Mandy are you okay? I know it's a shock and I wish I could have told you sooner or in person, but I didn't know where to find you. Nobody knew where you were, even Jason! I had to hire a tracing agency and they only managed to locate you now. That's how I managed to call you."
Silence.

"Mandy? Are you there? Oh God don't tell me this bloody phone has cut off again! Mandy?" she grumbled into the phone as I tried to answer.

"I'm here!" I whispered. The tears in my voice were betraying me. I wanted to be strong and show that I didn't care, but I did.

"You know they loved you, even after you left without saying good-bye. They tried to find you Mandy, but you made it hard for us all." I could hear her crying too.

"I'm sorry Ma! I'm so sorry!" I said as my sobs took over again. So much for being strong!

"Listen sweetheart, I need you to be strong now, okay?" she said, her grandmotherly instincts taking over. "I need you to be strong and I need you to come home my darling."

"What? No! No way! I can never come home Ma. Not after the way I left. Anyway, what's there to be done now? Mum and Dad must already be buried so what do you need me for?" I asked breathlessly, already knowing that Zoe would be top of my list of people that needed me.

"Mandy, you have to come home. It's time to stop hiding and come back. How soon can you come?" Just like Grandma to assume I could just pick up and go without a care in the world.

"I can't Ma.   I have responsibilities here."   Like Zachary!

"I have a job and I can't take leave without warning them." Any excuse would do right now.

"When I spoke to your boss, she said that you would be able to come home straight away Amanda! Don't lie to me now. I need you. Please come home, my darling!" her voice sounded tired and she had started crying again.

What could I do?   There was no way to avoid the inevitable and as much as I wanted to pick up and run, I had to think of Zach.   His little face, with those big brown eyes and cute dimples. I had to think of him too. It was time to stop hiding and go back to face the truth.

"Okay Ma." I sighed. "I'll be there as soon as I can."

CHAPTER THREE

Jennifer stared at me as I sat across from her in her office. The autumn sun was blazing down and shone on her hair, turning it into a golden halo that didn't match her not-so-heavenly expression.

"I know that you have family commitments in Zimbabwe Amanda, but you have to realise that I need your help right now and we are understaffed as it is." She grimaced and sat back on her chair. Opening the file in front of her she scanned through the notes and telephone messages left on top of the correspondence. "I need you to keep working, even though you are going back home. Do you think you could balance your personal life and continue to support our firm?" she asked, looking up with blue eyes holding a question that needed no answer.

"Of course Jennifer. What is it you want me to do?" I asked, intrigued at how I could help all the way in Zimbabwe when I knew that we had no contacts there.

Just then there was a knock on Jennifer's main door and Em peaked her head around the door.

"Sorry to interrupt Jennifer, but you asked me to send Mr Edwards through as soon as he arrived. He is here now." She smiled, her eyes watching me.

"Yes, please send him in Emma. Thank you!" Jennifer dismissed her with a wave of her thin, blue veined hand.

I blinked in confusion. I thought we were discussing the terms of my taking time off to go home. Why was Jennifer seeing a client now? I stood up preparing to gather the notebook and pencil I always carried into her office in case she wanted me to take down correspondence in short hand for a client's file. She looked up and gestured for me to stay. There was a sound behind me and I turned to see Mr Edwards enter Jennifer's office. My face heated until I felt it was beetroot red. Mr Edwards was the same client I had encountered in the reception area the day I had received the news about my parents!

His eyes held a steely grimness as he gazed at Jennifer and then he noticed me standing next to the other visitor's chair and there was a faint glimmer of recognition.

"Mr Edwards, thank you for coming back at such short notice," Jennifer said, giving a thin lipped smile that never reached her piercing blue eyes. "Please sit down and we can discuss the arrangements. Amanda, please take your seat."

We both complied and I could feel tension building in me as I sat only a few inches from him. He was wearing

24

a coal black suit that seemed to bring out the darkness of his eyes and hair. His skin had a soft golden glow to it and his hands had remarkably long fingers with slightly marked scars over the knuckles. It seemed strange for a man so well dressed to have hands that looked roughened from labour. Maybe he was a self-made man and contrived his fortune through hard work. The nails were perfect if not smudged at the cuticle, as though they were scrubbed but could never erase the work they had done. I glanced up and caught him watching me with the same expression of amusement I had seen at our previous encounter. With my face heating up again, I tried to pull off a friendly smile and turned my attention to Jennifer who was going over the file in front of her again and thankfully did not notice my unprofessionalism.

"Well, as I was explaining to Amanda just before you arrived Alex, we have some business we need completed in Harare and as you both will be travelling there, I thought we could kill two birds with one stone and get you two to complete the assignment together."

I didn't dare glance to my left to see Alex Edward's expression but his deep voice filled the room with a timber tone that set my insides alight with little currents.

"What exactly is the assignment Jennifer?" he asked, leaning slightly forward.

"We have a client who purchased property in Zimbabwe, but decided to live here in the UK. The government is passing a new law that supports tenants in claiming properties where the landlords have emigrated to another country. I need you to go there and find out exactly what rights our client has to fight any claims to his properties. I will need you to work with one of the law firms there as we have no jurisdiction to act if there are any law suits. I expect you to wrap up the property if you see a threat and we can assist the client in retrieving any funds from the sale." She flicked through the file and passed it to Alex.

"Make sure that you cover all bases as our client is a major player. We do not want any mistakes as he brings in 40% of our earnings in land registries," she pointed out, a thin smile appearing. "Book your flights for the end of this week and you have a month to complete your assignment. Amanda will be there assist you, but she has some personal business to attend to as well."

Alex glanced at me, a question in his eyes. I just smiled back and turned my attention to business.

"Will you require immediate updates for the client or will weekly reports be sufficient?" I asked. I had to make sure I covered all bases before I left.

"Yes, weekly updates should be sufficient. But be careful. The government there have a fickle way of doing business and if they can get a back payment from you, they will. Don't trust anyone!" Jennifer said and stood up, as if dismissing us. "Liaise with each other on travel and accommodation arrangements and I'm sure Amanda will sort out the details." She moved to her cupboard and pulled out her coat and tan briefcase. "I will not be in the office for the rest of this week so safe travels and I will hear from you once you are set up. Good luck!"

With that she walked out of the adjoining door to my office and said something to Emma before walking down the long corridor and out to the lifts. I turned to retrieve my notebook and pencil and looked up to find dark eyes staring at me again.

"Hi! I'm Amanda! I'll be booking the flights for Thursday evening if that's okay so that we can have an overnight flight and be there by morning." I was a little breathless after that sentence and yet, he just smiled and said nothing. Feeling a little flustered that I had to fill in the silence I gabbled on. "If there is any preference on where you would like to stay please inform me soon, as I have to book the hotel and make sure we have taxis and such."

He took a step closer to me. My heart started to race. Why was I so affected by this man? He was tall. Taller than most of the men at the firm and definitely better looking! I tried to find my cold, detached look but it was unavailable. Why was I so breathless? He just stared at me and lifted his hand towards my face. I clenched my fingers around my notepad, holding it close to my chest. With a gentle brush against my cheek, he slowly took a wayward curl that had come undone from the clips in my hair and curled it behind my ear.

"No dripping scarf today I see!" he said, blasting me with a smile that made my toes curl. He had deep dimples like Zachary and beautiful white teeth. I could feel myself blushing again and I shuffled back, feeling the chair catching on my trouser leg. I was trapped between the chair and Jennifer's desk.

He seemed to move slightly forward again, closing the already small space between us with his large frame. My insides were turning to jelly, and I felt like running out of the room, but couldn't move my legs. I took a deep breath to steady my nerves and could smell his expensive cologne.

"I recall the last time we met, you ran off after dripping all over my shoes," he said. His smile was accompanied by a raised eyebrow. He leaned even further towards me and I started to lean back, having nowhere to run. His left hand reached out as though to touch my face again but he leaned past me and retrieved another file from Jennifer's desk. I could feel the warmth from his body and my own treacherous body reacted as though he had stroked me. My jelly legs were losing their supportiveness, and I leaned against the desk to hold myself up.

"Sorry! I just need to get this file and you were in my way," he said, a wicked smile playing on his lips. He knew the effect he was having on me and was enjoying my discomfort.

Letting out the breath I had taken in and held onto when he had come closer, I stepped forward towards him and made my escape between the two visitor's chairs we had sat in just minutes ago. With a bit of distance, I regained my composure and turned to give him a smile full of confidence I did not feel.

"As I said, if there is anything else you would like me to organise for our trip, don't hesitate to contact me."

With as much elegance as I could muster, I moved to the door and walked out as though nothing untoward had just happened. Well, nothing had happened, but the way my body was reacting I felt as though I had been touched by this man! I quickly shut the door that adjoined my office to Jennifer's and leaned against it as though afraid he would follow me. Emma looked up at me with a quizzical expression. Just then Alex must have walked out of the other office door and down the corridor. She raised both her eyebrows and made a low wolf whistle only I could hear.

"Wow, that is one hot looking man!" she exclaimed and turned to look at me again. The eyebrows went up. "What exactly happened in the office?" she asked, a naughty smile crinkling her pert nose.

"Nothing! Just a little breathless is all!" I lied and quickly walked to my desk to start the booking process.

"I would be breathless too if I just spent a couple of minutes in an empty office with a hunk like that," she giggled. Before she could ask any more questions, her phone rang and I pretended to be very busy with my bookings.

The week flew by and before I knew it, the day for our travel to Zimbabwe had arrived. I had Emma's promise to check on the house or stay there over weekends. We were on a flight back to a country I never planned to return to; Zimbabwe. The land of the sun, wild beauty and extreme hardship, and a past that could destroy me.

Heathrow Airport was packed with people bustling to destinations around the world, voices over intercoms giving messages no-one could decipher and boards flickering with flight details and gate numbers. Zachary looked up at me with wonder in his eyes. He was tired as it had been a busy day of packing and trying to explain to him again and again why we had to leave our house and go to a different country to meet strangers. In the end, I found it easier to tell him that work was sending us on a special holiday. His five year old brain seemed to accept this and further questions on why dried up to be replaced with questions on what we would see, how big was the plane and where we would stay!

Alex Edwards was standing at the check-in counter as arranged, and his expression changed from the sultry smile to outright shock when he spied my little man standing next to me. Jennifer obviously had not bothered to tell him and I certainly did not give away any personal details about my trip. Quickly recovering his initial shock, he smiled and bent down to Zach's level, reaching out a hand to ruffle his hair.

"Hi! I'm Alex! What's your name little man?" he asked, crouching at eye level with Zach. He glanced up at me with an expression that I couldn't decipher, but drew his attention back to my bewildered son standing in front of him, staring.

"His name is Zachary," I said, keeping my face as expressionless as possible. If he wanted to know more, he would have to ask the questions. "Zach, say hi to Mr Edwards. He is coming with us on our trip. Remember I told you that my work will be sending us on a special holiday? Well, Mr Edwards will be coming too."

Zachary looked at me and then at Alex Edwards. We could see him turning over the information in his mind and he seemed to take his time over it. A little smile appeared on his face and his dimples appeared.

"Hi!" he said, holding out his hand to shake Alex's. Alex gave a little laugh as he offered his hand.

"You're going to look after my mummy and me! Will you let me ride on an elephant? Mummy said no, but I told her I would be careful. Oh, and can we go see the lions? Mummy said they keep them in a special place where we can see them. Can we go now?" His bright eyes were alight with excitement. He had forgotten to give Alex's hand back.

"Yes!" Alex replied, smiling at him and then he looked up at me. "I'm here to look after your mummy and you. And maybe we can see about riding an elephant and feeding lions! But first, let's get checked in and find our aeroplane to take us there." He smiled at me, dazzling me with his dark twinkling eyes and gorgeous smile. I felt my chest tighten and busied myself with finding the tickets and passports.

Why did this man get under my skin so easily? I had numerous men giving me looks and making flirty comments, but with Alex, I wanted to believe him. I wanted him to look after me and wrap his strong arms around me. His strong hands could hold mine and touch me anytime. What was I thinking? It was crazy to feel this way for a stranger whom I had to work with and could make this trip extremely awkward.

Shaking my head to try to clear it and push down all the emotions running through me I looked down at Zachary. He was still chatting to Alex who had stayed crouched at his level and held his own in a conversation about which was the best team in Hot Wheels! I sighed. Wouldn't it be easy to dream and have a man in my life to be a father to Zach? He did have a father, and I left him. His father was married now and chances were, I was going to see him.

Would it be too much to wish that Jason and Lola had moved to another town or country? It was bad enough I had to face my past but to face Jason and tell him he had a son would be awful. To see him with his new family, Lola, and however many kids he had would kill me. I had to keep Zach a secret for as long as possible.

If we wrapped up business quickly and I sorted Esther and Zoe out, I could be back to my safe England within a few weeks. I'm sure I could do it. I just had to get Alex on my side and get him to work double time. Then we could both be home safe and sound.

CHAPTER FOUR

The world had changed. Everything was bright and hot. The air itself seemed to buzz with life and the noise of crowded passengers shouting around us was deafening after the cool flight. I tried to hold onto Zachary, but the passengers shoving to get through passport control were shuffling us apart and my fingers couldn't hold on to our bags and his hand. Suddenly, Alex appeared next to us and he lifted Zachary up into his arms. Zach's eyes grew wide with uncertainty, and without another thought, he put his head on Alex's shoulder and wrapped his arms around the man's neck. I stared, my mouth dropping open. A shove in my back propelled me forward. Stumbling I grasped at the arm wrapping itself around my waist and holding me tight. Alex looked down at me, his eyes sent mixed signals as he squeezed me closer.

"Stay close to me and we'll get out of here soon. Can you hold your bags or do you want me to carry them?" he asked, looking at my load and assessing whether I could manage.

"I... I'm fine thank you. Are you sure you can handle Zach?" I asked, hoping the doubt I felt about him carrying Zach didn't come through as an insult.

He gave me a dimpled grin. "I think I can handle him. The poor little guy is tired and doesn't need the hassle of being pushed in this crowd." Looking around, his hand still around my waist squeezed me tighter to his side and he ushered me forward through a small gap in the chaotic surroundings. With his guidance we made it to the counter and had our documents stamped within minutes and on through to reclaim our larger suitcases.

Alex gave a quick whistle to a porter standing close by with his trolley and instructed him on which bags to collect from the carousal. Once the bags were collected, Alex pushed us forward again towards the wide glass doors opening out to a blue sky and the intense heat I hadn't felt for many years. The semi-coolness of the inside of the building compared to scorching heat was lost in seconds and the glare of the white airport building blinded us for a few seconds, until our eyes accustomed themselves to the reflective glare.

With his hand still around my waist, Alex guided me forward towards a waiting taxi. He had the porter load our things in the boot. He opened the passenger door and gently put Zachary inside, stepping aside so that I could follow. Once in, the door was closed and he went around the car to the front passenger seat, stopping to tip the porter and instruct our driver where to go. We would be staying at the Meikles hotel in the city centre. It was the best hotel in Harare, and thoroughly deserved its five star rating.

The taxi pulled out of the crowded entrance and made its way towards the main road leading out of the airport. With the windows open and fresh air blowing into the car, my hair blew around my face, sending curls everywhere. Zachary was still asleep, lying next to me on the seat. I glanced up to see Alex watching me with his coal black eyes and an expression that sent sparks down my spine. I could feel the heat of the day seeping into my skin, reminding me of my childhood and re-awakening thoughts and feelings from my past that I had kept hidden for so many years. Alex could never know the person I was or he would save those heart stopping smiles for someone else. Not me.

He grinned, oblivious to my inner turmoil and turned to see where the driver was pointing out some local spots of interest. I knew them all and watched his fascination over the balancing rocks and vast open vleis. Alex did not know I was from Zimbabwe. He thought I had distant family that lived here and I was to visit them. A reunion of sorts. That was what I had told him. I didn't know if Jennifer had informed him that my parents had been killed in a car crash and I was returning home to see the grandmother and sister I had left behind.

'The City of Harare Welcomes You' sign stood out on the side of the wide open road and I looked out of the window in time to see the Hatfield shopping centre. Nothing had changed. Cars were parked in front of burglar barred shop windows and people either loitered

on the pavements or in front of the bottle store, drinking and laughing. Tinny music blared out from one of the shop's open doors, or maybe it was the car parked close to the girls giggling at whatever jokes the young men standing close to them were telling.

The roads were in a pretty good condition, or was it just the straight Airport road leading from the airport to the city centre that was repaired? It would be something the government would do to entice visitors under false pretence. The smell of red dirt was prominent amongst a mixture of over-ripe fruit, heat and dust. I hadn't missed the smell or the dry earth with brittle brown tufts of grass suffering under the intense late October sun. Pretty soon, the long open road gave way to more intersections and traffic lights with the build-up of more houses and tall office blocks. Harare's City Centre opened up before us, a metropolis of honking horns, cars, buses with pedestrians fighting for the right to use the same streets.

Cars pulled into the street in front of us without looking and the taxi driver had to apply emergency brakes frequently, using his horn to show his frustration and lots of hand gestures accompanied by swear words in Shona that I vaguely understood. Zachary was awoken by the hooting and braking and was soon sitting on my lap looking out the window at the strange sights. His hair was damp with sweat and the back of his t-shirt stuck to his overheated body.

The majority of the people on the street were dressed smartly and bustled to and fro to their destinations. We could see the difference in the population immediately with the majority of the people milling about being black and only a few scatterings of white or coloured people milling about, some dressed in suits and other in casual jeans or shorts. Everything was loud; the traffic, the people talking to each other, so much so that we could capture bits of their conversation and their different accents.

With a swift turn to the left on Jason Moyo Avenue, we entered a side road that was not so busy and had trees cooling the pavements filled with pedestrians. We pulled into the curved sweep before a beautiful colonial building that screamed history and richness. It was the Meikles hotel in all its glory, surrounded by green shrubbery and a garden to the side. A doorman dressed in his long coat with shiny gold buttons and a smart cap opened the taxi doors for us and welcomed us. Alex gave him instructions about our bags and a porter magically appeared to collect them with his trolley.

We walked up the few steps and entered a marble foyer with sparkling lights and beautiful mahogany varnished wood giving an elegance and style to a smart desk perfectly placed to welcome visitors. A pretty young woman with beautiful smooth ebony skin stood behind the desk and welcomed us, and asked for our booking details.

I stepped forward, holding a still tired Zachary in my arms and answered that we were booked under Edwards and Glenson. She gave us a confused look and then smiled.

"Oh, I'm so sorry!" she said with a giggle. "I thought you were one family!"

"No, we are here on business," Alex answered, giving a smile that must have knocked her socks off. She lowered her long lashes and gave him a coy look.

"Well, let's hope there will be time for some pleasure too sir," she replied, a flirty smile showing her perfect set of white teeth. "Of course, there are many things to see, so all work and no play is not a good thing!" she continued, spying the expression on my face.

Alex grinned at me and I felt the heat back on my face. I didn't want him to think I cared, so I quickly answered, "Of course, this is a country of great beauty. It would be a waste not to see a bit of it before we return home."

The hotel receptionist smiled politely and finished processing our details. She handed out the key cards and informed us that we would have the deluxe suites. We thanked her politely and made our way to the lift. I shifted Zachary to the other side of my body, feeling his sweaty limbs and dead weight. This heat was not doing him any favours and he seemed lethargic. Suddenly, I felt a large pair of strong hands lift him out of my arms.

"Don't worry, I'll carry him up. This heat can't be good for him after the cold we left behind in England." Alex stepped through the lift's open doors and made space for me. "We had better make sure we keep him topped up on fluids in case he dehydrates," he continued, as though talking to himself.

I didn't know what to say. I just followed and stared at the buttons on the panel in front of me. The shine of the metal and the mirrors surrounding us gave me a view of the state of my hair and face. I looked tired and my hair had come undone from the bun I had made, sending brown curls around my face and down my back. I gave them a quick swish to try and push them into some attractive semblance of order, but they stubbornly fell back, forming a frame of wayward curls around my face. My green eyes looked too big and my lips were pale without any gloss or colour. Frightful! As though reading my mind, Alex smiled and reached out to gently put a curl behind my ear.

"I think you need a rest too. It was a long flight and we still have to contact the local lawyers that we are going to be working with. Why don't you and Zach have a nap and we'll meet up again for an early dinner?"

"Sure. That's sounds fine. Would you like me to order up some lunch for you? Or would you like me to contact the lawyers and let them know that we're here?" I asked, trying to sound professional under my grotty exterior. I still had to complete a job and the sooner I did that, the sooner we could return to England.

"No, don't worry. I'll do that," he said. "Just have a rest for today and we'll get started tomorrow. I'm sure they will be willing to make a special arrangement to meet us on a Saturday," he continued.

The lift pinged and opened onto the 10th floor. The hall led to a small number of doors on either side of the foyer and our rooms were located toward the right. Alex took the key cards out of his pocket and opened the first door, standing to one side to let me go in first. The room was spacious and airy, furnished in soft pastel blues, pinks and greens with Maplewood furnishings and a rather large double bed, a small sofa and chairs by the window and a desk with a comfortable seat against one wall. There was a door slightly ajar which gave us a glimpse of a luxurious bathroom with fluffy white towels. Next to the large built in cupboards was a small junior bed, just perfect for Zach. There was a little coffee table with pamphlets and menus.

Alex gently lay Zach on the double bed and started taking off his shoes. I put my bag down on the end of the bed and came to assist him. Our fingers brushed each other as we untied the second shoe and I dropped it as though it was on fire! His dark eyes searched my face and I could feel his breath blowing wisps of hair that fell across my eyes. Zachary gave a little sigh and seemed to slip into a deeper slumber now that he was lying peacefully on a cool, comfortable surface.

Slowly we both straightened up and stood so close, I could feel my heart jumping out of my chest to meet his. I had to look up to see his strong jaw, a five 'o clock shadow highlighting his high cheekbones and adding a hardness to his expression that sparked a slow shiver down my spine. His fingers trailed a slow path up my arms and I held my breath. Reaching forward, our lips met in a soft kiss, gently melting into each other with a warmth that reached the core of my being. We drew closer, our bodies touching and without a conscious thought, my hands were wrapped around his narrow waist, feeling the sinuous muscles in his back.

Heat flushed through me with a savage lick of its tongue and my body flared as fire coursed through it at rocket speed. His hand reached into my hair and pulled at the elastic holding it in its messy bun, setting it free to fall cascade down my shoulders and back. I sighed, leaning into him and feeling every pore awaken as his arousal stroked against me through the thin material separating our flesh.

A loud knock at the door shocked me out of my dream state and I jumped back, out of his warm embrace. What was I doing? I quickly ran a hand through my hair and stepped back again. I was making my life more complicated than I needed it to be. I didn't know this man, didn't know whether he was in a relationship or if he had kids of his own. I was kissing a stranger as passionately as I would an old lover and considering what little experience I had in that department, the shame washed over me.

The knock at the door was more insistent and I jumped. I frowned. Who was that? Oh, the porter with our bags. Alex just stood there, next to the bed with my son sleeping peacefully, and watched the emotions playing across my face. His eyes were hard unreadable orbs, but I could see the muscle on the side of his jaw working.

"Don't over think things Mandy," he said, his deep voice caressing my name. I realised this was the first time he had called me by my name, my nickname. It felt good!

Alex walked over to let the porter deliver in. I had to get busy and not let him think that the kiss had affected me so deeply. But it had. I had never ever been kissed so intensely. Jason had never touched any part of me and our coupling had been a brief interlude with aggressive groping and sloppy kisses. I still cringed at the memory. It was incredible to think that the product from such a brief encounter could be so perfect and innocent. I looked down at my baby boy lying on the bed as I felt the effects of the kiss on my lips and deep down in places I had only been touched once before. The need to hold onto reality worked through the tingles. Alex and I had to work together and I couldn't afford to dabble in a relationship that could not last. It would not be fair on Zach and he was my number one concern.

All these years my reputation of being aloof and unapproachable helped protect me from the dating pool at work. I couldn't bear to see Zachary getting close to a man, only to see him leave a gaping hole in his life. It was bad enough I couldn't tell Zach about his real father and avoided talking about him. My excuses that his dad was far away and we could never reach him were thin and wouldn't work forever. Now Alex had broken through a barrier I had kept to protect us from a world where questions would have to be answered about Zachary's father. Would the kiss be worth the pain of him leaving me when he found out the truth about my past?

CHAPTER FIVE

Saturday morning arose with the glorious October sun. The warmth could be felt and seen as soon as the heavily draped curtains were drawn back. I stood there, blinded for a minute, taking in the brightness glistening through the soft netting that afforded us some privacy from the bustling streets below. This was Harare at its finest. Residents of the town always rose early on a Saturday and the shops happily supported their custom by opening at 8.00am.

By lunch time, the main street would have calmed to a slow murmur as the heat beat down on quiet streets and people took cover to enjoy a relaxing lunch and afternoon siesta, until the coolness of the evening would draw out those seeking night time entertainment at local bars and restaurants. Though the economy had suffered such brutal attacks from poor governing and a loss of the Zimbabwe dollar to the point where it was all but worthless and other foreign currency, mainly the US dollar was used instead, the peoples' habits remained the same. Live for today; for who knows if we will still be around tomorrow!

Alex and I had joined the evening crowd for an early dinner. Many locals enjoyed coming to the Meikles for drinks before a night out and some dined at the five star restaurants in the hotel itself. We chose to dine in a smaller restaurant, just off the main lobby area where the tables were set with simple but exquisite white tablecloths mixed with gold and red overlays. Crystal chandeliers offered a soft ambience to the room and waiters in starched white shirts and colourful waistcoats waited on us with a warmth and friendliness I had not encountered in years.

Once seated, I took the opportunity to start questioning the mysterious Alex Edwards whom I had only known for less than a week and yet had made such a difference to my emotional state.

"So Alex, where are you from?" I asked, sipping a crisp, cool chardonnay before our meal was served.

"Well, I have been around the world and stayed in many different places. I was originally from South Africa, but my work made me travel to many countries. England has been home for quite a few years now," he said, a smile hovering. "What other burning questions do you want to ask me?" His dimples creased the sides of his mouth and his high cheekbones stood out, magnifying his straight black eyebrows with hooded dark eyes that twinkled at me.

"I would like to know how you started working at Alann and Cook, and what it is you actually do," I replied, not really interested in his answer. I wanted to ask if he was married, had children, a girlfriend and a serious relationship! Those would have to wait till later, once the chardonnay had given me a bit more courage!

"Alann and Cook have hired me to help sort out the problem with the Partels. I was only hired recently. In fact, the same day you decided to drip all over my new Gucci shoes!" he laughed. "I will help sort this problem out here in Zimbabwe and then once we return to England, I'm afraid it will be back to my own company."

He was not going to stay at the same company I worked for and that meant it would not conflict with my work ethics. Was I making excuses for my loose behaviour with him? Obviously! But I needed to make it right in my mind, if there was something between us. Zach had asked for him as soon as he woke and I had to reassure my little boy that he would see Alex again the next morning. I could see my son's heart losing itself to a stranger and as much I as wanted to stop him, my heart was following suit. It gave me the courage to do something I tried to keep down to a minimum in England. I hired the in-house baby-sitter so that I could join Alex for dinner without having to worry about Zach asking his own set of probing questions.

"Are you married Alex?"

"I was many years ago. Unfortunately, my wife died in an accident before we had a chance to start a family."

His expression changed and hooded eyes shut down with a hardness in them whilst the muscle in his cheek worked furiously. He obviously did not want to talk about it. Silence descended over our table and my heart sank. So much for probing questions.

"What about you Amanda Glenson? Where are you from? How long have you worked at Alann and Cook and I assume you are not married?"

"Umm yeah ... I have lived in England for quite a while and had Zachary. He's five and has started school. I've worked for the firm for about five or six years now and no, I'm not married!" I answered.

"So where were you before moving to England? Do you have family there?" he asked, eyeing the waiter approaching with our salmon soufflé starters. I took the opportunity of the distraction not to answer and accepted the food and subtly changed the subject to favourite foods.

The evening progressed amicably and Alex was great company. His world view made him interesting to chat to and he had many funny anecdotes about the places he had visited. I kept up my end of the conversation with my knowledge of the history of the places and the evening came to an end far sooner than I had expected. We stood outside the hotel room door and I hesitated before inserting my key card to give me access to the bedroom. I knew Zachary would be fast asleep and the baby sitter would be watching television. Alex stepped closer to me and I held my breath in anticipation.

"Whatever our histories Mandy, I think we may have a chance to start something new here. I hope you're as keen as I am," he said and leaned in for a kiss which was gentle yet demanding. I responded and held his arms which had encircled me in a loose hug. With a peck on my nose he walked down to his door and waved goodnight.

The startling sound of the phone ringing pulled me out of my reverie of the night before. I quickly went over to answer it before it awakened Zachary. It was the front desk asking if I wanted my breakfast delivered to my room immediately or in fifteen minutes. After informing them fifteen minutes would be fine, I quickly jumped into the shower to get ready for the business of the day. I had to attend the meeting with the lawyers this morning to establish what was required to secure the Partel's property and I also had to phone Esther, my grandmother, to meet her later in the day. My heart leapt at the thought of seeing my family again. It was going to be a long day!

Once dressed and fed, Zachary and I were downstairs in the lobby waiting for Alex by 9.00am. I had called Esther to arrange to meet her at her house in Belvedere later in the afternoon. She still did not know I had Zachary with me. I guess we were all in for a surprise. Alex came to meet us downstairs in the foyer and a smile hovered on his lips as Zachary immediately spotted him and ran to him as though he was seeing his best friend after many years. Alex's eyes sparkled for a second and his smile beamed down at Zach before he swept him up into his arms and gave him a huge hug.

"Hiya buddy! Did you sleep well?" he asked, holding Zach in the crook of his arm whilst Zach hugged him around his broad shoulders.

"Uh huh! I thought I would see you at breakfast Alex," was my smart mouthed son's reply. I had the decency to blush when Alex looked at me and raised an eyebrow.

"Well, I had to get ready too. But we're all here now. Are you ready to go to some boring meetings with us and then have some fun?" he asked, smiling at my little boy's eager nod and another squeezy hug.

A pang of jealousy ran through me. As a single mother, most of my special moments were filled with anxiety about travel, finance and looking after a little boy on my own. It left little time for uninhibited joy. I felt the sorrow of knowing that I had kept Zach away from a father figure to make him feel secure. Not that Zachary lacked anything in his life. Seeing Zachary hug Alex and converse in such an adult tone made me see my son in a different light. At some point I would have to tell him about his father and give him a chance to know him. If his father was interested, that is.

The porter came in to tell us our taxi was waiting outside and we made our way into the lovely hot sunny day from the coolness of the Meikles hotel foyer. The heat permeated through my soft georgette blouse and pooled around my thighs under my pencil skirt. I was grateful for choosing strappy sandal-type heels instead of the enclosed court shoes which would have made my feet sweat in agony. Luckily the offices of Mohammed, Ismail and Co. were not too far away and it took us about ten minutes through the morning traffic to arrive at the blue glass fronted Karigamombe Centre. Its shiny exterior and sharp edged design reflected the sun and gave off an astounding blue hue onto the neighbouring buildings as we travelled along the marbled entrance to the lifts and up to the 10th floor. The view afforded us was spectacular and we could see as far as the Zimbabwe national flame which was straight down Samora Machel Avenue and many miles out of town.

Mr Ismail was a rather short tubby man with glasses teetering at the end of his bulbous nose. He reminded me of garden gnome, but was warm and welcoming and soon had us settled in his luxurious office with more amazing views of the city.

"I hope your flight was alright and you are not too jet lagged," he said, his warm smile threatening to pull his glasses further down his nose. "We have been the lawyers for the Partel family for many years," he continued in a singsong voice, "and unfortunately, now that they have decided to move away, it puts their properties at risk."

"We were made aware of only one property that needed our attention Mr Ismail," Alex replied. "How many properties are there altogether and what exactly is the status of things at the moment?"

Mr Ismail explained the situation in great detail. I quickly made notes of what we were required to do. Zachary played quietly by the floor to ceiling window. He was tracing the outlines of the palm tree tops seen in abundance down below and the tops of the buildings, some not much taller than the trees.

"What is the estimated timeline you foresee us needing to stay to sort it out?" Alex asked.

"Well, with the given tasks at hand and the fact that sometimes the courts can take their time to process deeds, I estimate about a month or more!" replied Mr Ismail. I smiled at him as he looked at me and then Zachary. "Will you be staying at the hotel for that length of time?" he asked kindly, obviously taking in the fact that we had a little boy with us. "It is not often we get to see a family travel together to do business. I like it. In fact, I can offer you one of my houses to stay in instead of a stuffy hotel. That way, you can rest assured that whatever length of time it takes to finalise this business, it will not stress you out as a family."

I stuttered, trying to find an appropriate answer to such a generous offer.

"No! No! Please don't argue with me!" he continued over our protests. "I insist! It is far better for a child to be in a home than in a cold hotel room for so long. In fact we could enrol him in a local school whilst he is here and that will give you both enough time to run around as there will be a lot of travelling during the day to view the properties."

"Mr Ismail, that is very kind, but I must insist we stay ..."

"Thank you Mr Ismail. We accept! It will be better for Zachary and much more comfortable than a stuffy hotel. Please rest assured we will repay you for any expenses!" Alex butted in before I could protest further. I frowned at him, giving him an abrasive look that hopefully said I didn't like him taking the decision upon himself of where we stayed. And he hadn't corrected Mr Ismail about our relationship.

"Don't worry about a thing. I'll have my wife open the house up and it will be stocked with food for the next couple of weeks so you don't have to worry about finding the supermarket just yet, hahaha!" he laughed, his rotund middle shaking like a jellybean.

With that, he stood up and shook Alex's hand and mine and then came round his desk to shake Zachary's hand, who looked quite confused with all the adults smiling at him. Mr Ismail gave his cheek a little pinch and asked him if he liked school. Zachary nodded mutely and Mr Ismail told him that he would meet many friends at his new school that he would be visiting soon. Zach's eyes grew big and he looked at me with an excitement that told me I would have no choice but to send him to the school and answer a million more questions.

CHAPTER SIX

After the meeting was over, I slumped into the taxi, hot and bothered with the turn of events. Living in a house would mean closer proximity to Alex. That would leave Zach and I open to falling in love with this man further. Things were moving too fast and I felt like a huge wave, a tsunami, was hitting the shores of my life. I couldn't seem to keep up with making the right decision. Run from it, or swim?

Alex was sure of himself, but he didn't know me. He didn't know my past and I still had to face that myself. There was no way I could look at a future until I managed to sort things out. That meant facing up to what I had run from and taking the blame for it, no matter what the consequences. It could open up the possibilities of losing Zachary in the process.

I felt dark eyes watching me from the rear view mirror and looked up to find Alex's eyes observing my reaction. He frowned slightly and his fiery eyes sparked with irritation at my reaction.

"We had better sort ourselves out in terms of communication and transport. Can you drive?" he asked sharply. I nodded, unable to speak and not trusting myself not to burst into tears with all the emotional turmoil I felt. I hugged tightly onto Zach and he squirmed in my arms, protesting that he was hot. Alex

56

told the driver to take us to the nearest mobile phone store and then on to a car hire.

By lunchtime we were set up with a rental car and two new mobile phones and our bags were packed into the boot ready to go to Mr Ismail's house. We would be living on the outskirts of the Central Business District in one of the more affluent neighbourhoods called Avondale.

It was a beautiful neighbourhood with avenues filled with jacaranda trees, arching over the quiet roads, forming a pretty canopy of green mixed with purple flowers. We had access to a private hospital close by, supermarkets with local produce in abundance and a movie theatre. There were only two or three shopping malls in Harare and they were small in comparison to the ones found in England. Notwithstanding that, the quality of goods found in the malls were to rival the best stores in London as they sold original leather bags, shoes and clothing designed by artists renowned for their quality of workmanship around the world. Diamonds glistened in jewellery stores and gold was of a higher quality and at much cheaper prices than overseas.

The local supermarkets served the neighbourhoods and had huge parking lots surrounding many independent stores. At the Avondale shopping centre, they had a wonderful market every Saturday located behind the main buildings, overlooking open grassland. There was a big difference in the view, compared to England, where the backs of stores would be stuffed with dirty bins and dangerous alleyways. Harare boasted open grassland backing onto houses and shopping markets, all hand in hand showing the free land still unused and left for the Mupane and Eucalyptus trees to grow happily under the hazy blue sky.

Our new accommodation was situated behind the shops along a narrow lane called Bath Road. It had a broad gate with a large chain and lock. Beyond the driveway lay a sprawling bungalow with a red topped roof and white walls showing off large open windows secured with metal burglar bars, a common sight in nearly all the houses.

The house was surrounded by many trees, some of which I didn't recognise. I could hear the birds singing and squabbling above our heads, hidden from view amongst the variegated leaves. Alex pressed the car horn twice and a small, gangly African man ran to open the gate for us. He saluted as we drove in and we parked to the side of the house, adjacent to the kitchen door. A beautiful Indian woman came out into the sun and shielded her eyes with a heavily bejewelled hand.

"Hello, you must be Alex and Amanda!" she said, welcoming us in and bending to give Zachary a hug. "Hello mister! You must be the clever little Zach I heard all about!"

Zachary wiggled out of the hug, very unsure at the over-friendliness of this stranger. He hid behind my leg and held on for dear life. I laughed it off and greeted the lady that turned out to be Mr Ismail's wife. She showed us around the property which had three bedrooms, a rather large living room with an open brick fireplace and lovely pastel coloured walls giving each room a light airy feel. Beautiful French doors were opened out to the garden and a gentle wind blew the soft netting hanging across the windows. There was a yummy citrus smell and I could see a big bowl of fruit perched on a coffee table to the side of the overstuffed sofas.

The bedrooms were just as appealing and Zachary's appointed room was filled with soft toys and even a train set. He instantly settled down to play with the trains as we continued on our tour. The master bedroom was furnished in rich mahogany with a dark bedstead, big enough to hold at least four adults! I looked around and found wall to ceiling cupboards on one side of the room and an elegant dressing table with three way mirrors against the far wall. The third bedroom housed a simple double bed with soft furnishings in cool mint green and white furniture to compliment the built-in white wardrobes. I instantly fell in love with the bedroom with mint coloured carpet, dainty dressing table and window seat perfect to curl up and read a book. The curtains had tiny yellow flower details embroidered and a purely feminine aura encompassed the pretty room.

Once through the bedrooms we were led down the long passageway which gave access to the two bathrooms, and back to the kitchen which seemed overstocked with fruit bowls and packets of shopping.

"My husband said you were staying at the Meikles, so I did a little shopping for you to help settle you down. There is everything you need for your little boy in the larder and fridge and if you think of anything else, you can send Sonzo to the shops to buy it for you." She said, her lilting voice giving way to a heavier South African accent. Sonzo was the gardener that had opened the gate for us. He stayed in a small cottage to the side of the house. He would be in charge of the gardens and general housework and laundry.

"Thank you so much for your kindness Mrs Ismail. Allow us to invite you to dinner later this week once we have settled," I said, taking the hand offered as she said good-bye.

"We would love that!" she replied, adding, "And then I'll get to pinch your cute little boy's cheeks!"

With that, she was gone and we were left to our own devices. Packing the food took only a short time and Sonzo had brought in our suitcases, which I instructed him to put in the separate rooms. I did not want Alex getting any ideas on how far this so-called relationship was going and chose the green room which had the advantage of being opposite Zachary's room. Alex's things were place in the master bedroom. As soon as I saw the time, I knew I had to get away to meet my grandmother. I made an excuse of wanting to go to the local shops to see what they had to offer and before Alex had time to tell me he needed to make a few calls and set up an office in the dining room, I was out the door with Zachary in tow!

I knew the way to Ma's house and it felt like déjà vu travelling down the streets of Avondale leading on to Milton Park and then Belvedere. Each neighbourhood adjoined the other with wide open roads and traffic lights keeping order. Pedestrians walked slowly along the roadside and emergency taxis, the public transport system that was both dangerous and strangely efficient, swerved to an abrupt stop in front of side traffic to drop off passengers and pick up the stragglers waiting on the roadside for a lift to different destinations around town.

Esther Munford's house was halfway down Honey Drive. She lived just a few houses down from Jason's family home and I hoped that her servant would be fast and open the gate before anyone could see me waiting outside the gate. The house had not changed much since the last time I saw it and the sand-speckled walls surrounding the property glistened in the late afternoon sun whilst the austere gate remained shut for far too long. I hooted again, hoping that Kumbi had heard me this time and would come to open the locked gate.

Suddenly I heard a clanging sound as the lock opened and the chain were removed. The gate slowly opened on one side and a head appeared, peeking to see who was making such a noise. I smiled and waved my hand and Kumbi smiled in return, opening both sides of the gate so that I could drive through. Zachary stared with bright brown eyes at everything around him as though he was visiting Aladdin's cave. Fruit trees of all varieties lined the driveway on the left and on the right stood a large oak tree with a jasmine shrub curled around its trunk, leaving a sweet smell in the air as we drove past. The gate clanged shut behind us and I could see Kumbi running to the side of the house to alert my grandmother that I had arrived. There was no turning back now.

"Hi Ma!" I greeted my long lost grandmother, coming forward to hug her. She stood, staring at me as though I were an alien and robotically hugged me back. I turned to the side and brought Zachary out from behind me. "I'd like you to meet your great grandson Ma," I added, my voice sounding sheepish even to my own ears.

Ma's eyes opened wide as she stared down at her great grandchild. Tears welled up and she brushed them aside as she slowly bent down to cup Zachary's face with her gnarled hands. A little sob escaped her as Zach looked up and smiled, his bright brown eyes shining and his little teeth peeking out in a goofy grin.

"Oh my boy! My little boy!" she cried and swept him into her arms and proceeded to squeeze him till I had to gently prise him from her grip. "Sorry, sorry, I didn't mean to squeeze you so hard my boy," she said, tears still streaming down her face. "Why didn't you tell me Ma?" she asked, looking at me with sadness in her light hazel eyes.

She had changed so much. Gone was the confident, handsomely dressed grandmother I remembered growing up. Instead, an old lady in a floral dress stood in front of me with her shoulders slightly bent forward as though the world weighed too much and a deep sadness in her eyes that made my own eyes water whenever I stared into them. Her gnarled fingers looked as though they had been subjected to too much hard work and I wondered what could have happened to make a person look so different. Surely my father would have looked after Ma and made sure she was well established, even if they did not agree with the way she had brought me up?

"I'm so sorry Ma, but I just couldn't tell anyone. And by the time I knew myself, it was too late anyway," I replied, my hand holding her shoulder. Zachary hugged tightly onto me, afraid of the old lady that had squeezed him with so much love he would never understand. "I hope it's still okay Ma. I really wanted to see you and see Zoe too. Where is she?" I asked, hoping that Zoe would want to see me.

Ma's eyes clouded over and her face hardened. "Zoe is inside. You must understand that no-one blames you Mandy. I want you to understand that before you see Zoe, okay?"

"What do you mean? What happened to Zoe?" I asked, fear and panic rising in my throat.

"Well, remember the accident?" she asked, "Nobody knew that Zoe was in the factory at the time. Your dad couldn't remember if he sent her to fetch some papers. Unfortunately no-one knows how she escaped the fire and with the scars and memories, it has affected Zoe so much that she hasn't spoken since it happened."

My head couldn't take in all this information and I felt faint under the weight of Zachary and the news. It hit me hard to think that the fire I had mistakenly started years ago had nearly killed my own sister, let alone killing her rescuer.

"I need to sit down Ma, please," I begged, my legs giving way. "Can we go inside now?"

Ma led the way through the veranda and into the lounge which was rather dark from the brightness outside. It took my eyes a while to adjust and when they did, the shock of how my grandmother and sister were living hit me hard. The parquet flooring was covered by old carpets that had seen better days and furniture that was so mismatched and old, it looked as though it was out of a charity shop.

The solid pine dining suite that I remembered from when I was young was replaced by a simple kitchen table with a laminate cover and metal chairs. The sofas had sunken seats and little sprouts of fluff coming out of the sides as though the skin of the sofas had given way to war wounds. In the corner of the lounge was a tiny little television set, blaring out some local music with a tinny sound that annoyed the hell out of me.

Zoe sat on an armchair next to the television and she stared at the screen as though mesmerised by the dancing idiots displaying their gyrating hips to the tinny beat. At the sound of our entry she turned slightly to look at us and I gasped. Zoe's face was burnt from her left eye down to her neckline. It was an ugly deep burn that had twisted her skin where the heat had licked away at her cheek and looked grotesque in contrast to the other side which was smooth and strikingly beautiful. Her eyes took in my reaction and I could feel the hatred emanating from her, not only from her sneering mouth but from the way her fingers twisted around each other.

"Zoe ... I ... I didn't know. I am so sorry!" I stuttered, trying not to cry. The guilt I felt, the revulsion over my own stupidity. How could I have left my family and run away like a coward?

"No-one blames you ma," said my grandmother from behind me. She put her hand on my shoulder and squeezed it. "Remember it was an accident. Even the police finished their investigation and dropped all charges against you. You ran away before we could get the news to you. Mandy, I know that at the time it seemed like we were all against you, but you shouldn't have run away. We would have been there for you."

Her words were like ice on my heated brain. I looked at my sister and couldn't step closer to her, couldn't move in any direction with her laser stare fixated on me and then on Zachary. My brain threw me back five years into the past, taking me to the accident and the devastation after. The police had arrested me, claiming I was the culprit that had set the fire in the printing warehouse. Nobody believed me when I said I had been sent there by a strange phone call. No-one, not my parents, not Zoe, not even Jason had believed me when I told them that I had not been running away from the blaze but running to get help. After that, I had to escape from people that had no faith in me and were willing to let me rot in jail for something I didn't do. The final nail in the coffin was finding out I was pregnant, the same day that Jason announced his engagement to Lola. That was all I needed to speed my escape.

Zoe slowly got up from her chair and moved towards us. I tentatively took a step back, thinking she might hurt Zach, or me from the look in her eyes. Her face slowly crumpled into pain and tears and her arms reached out to hug us. I closed the gap between us and drew her in, my own tears blinding me.

"I'm so sorry Zoe, I didn't know" I repeated again and again. I held her close, feeling her shuddering sobs match mine and Zachary's who was confused and frightened by two crying women squeezing him in between.

Ma pushed between us and grabbed Zach rather roughly saying, "Hey you two! Enough now! You're frightening the child!"

Zach screamed in fear and scrambled to get back to me. I quickly grabbed hold of him and tried to comfort him.

"I'm sorry Ma. He's not used to any of this and it's such a big change. Give him a chance to get accustomed to you and Zoe and then he will be okay," I implored. A look of calmness took over Ma's face and she smiled gently at Zach.

"Sorry sweetheart. We didn't mean to frighten you. So your name is Zachary! You can call me Ma and this is your Aunty Zo Zo! You're going to see a lot of us now that you are home my boy and you can be spoilt rotten by your Ma, okay?" she said.

Without waiting for a response, she turned and walked towards the kitchen, calling out for Kumbi to make some cool drinks for us. I turned back to Zoe who was gently stroking the back of Zach's hand. She smiled at me, a Jekyll and Hyde sort of smile; beautiful on one side with a grimace on the other half of her face. It was so hard not to stare, but she didn't seem to mind. I suppose she was so used to it by now, it didn't affect her as much.

She beckoned to me to come and sit with her on one of the stuffed sofas and I gently put Zach between us. He seemed to stare at Zoe for long periods and then look around as if in disbelief that he was sitting there, in such a place, with a scarred woman beside him, stroking his hand again. She made a sign to me as though asking where I had been. I slowly retold the story of how I had left straight after the fight with Mum and Dad, their voices raised in anger and their disappointment filtering into harsh words. I hadn't known then that Zoe was in hospital, my own world turned upside down by the news of me being charged with arson. Dad's business had taken a severe beating from the fire and they were trying to get the insurers to rule out arson from a family member so that they could be paid out and start afresh.

Zoe looked at me, a frown on her face and I couldn't make out what she was thinking. We had been very close as children. We were inseparable and yet, as teenagers, Zoe seemed to distance herself from me with each passing day. I guess my guilt was making excuses for me leaving my sister to her own pain after I made a coward's escape, running away from my responsibilities.

Just then, I heard a car drive up and park on the stones close to my rented Toyota Corolla. Oh no, who could be coming to visit now? Zoe seemed to sense my panic and put a hand over my arm. She smiled slightly, as though the visitor was someone she knew well. I could hear the approaching footsteps and turned to see a well-built figure walk through Ma's front door. His brown eyes flashed with surprise and his expression turned from confusion to anger and then to curiosity as he looked at the little boy sitting next to me. It was Jason!

CHAPTER SEVEN

"Hello Jason," I said, standing up and strategically placing my body in front of Zachary.

"Umm, hi!" he replied, running a hand through his curly brown hair. I could see the muscles flexing under his shirt sleeves and the agitated way he slightly pulled his hair. "What are you doing here Mands?"

"I had to come back. Umm…Ma contacted me and told me that Dad and Mummy were in an accident," I said, speaking to him as though the many years had not passed.

"They died six month ago Mands," he replied, a frown creasing his handsome forehead. "Is that your little boy?"

"Uh, yes!" I squeaked, turning and gesturing to Zach who seemed quite content to sit next to Zoe now that another stranger had appeared. "This is Zachary, my little boy!"

Jason looked at him and smiled. "He's cute. So where's the father?"

Just then, Ma came back into the room with Kumbi in tow, carrying a tray containing a plate of biscuits and glasses filled with juice and ice cubes clinking merrily in the silence. They looked very appealing to my dry throat. Kumbi put the tray down on the large coffee table in the centre of the room and left without looking up. Ma greeted Jason with a hug and a kiss and he plonked himself in the armchair where Zoe had been sitting before, reaching over to switch off the television. Drinks were handed out and I swigged mine, enjoying the coolness as it slid down my parched throat. Jason politely refused his glass, choosing instead to stare intently at Zachary with a permanent crease to his brow. We all sat down and I could feel the tension seeping into my pores as everyone looked at me, as though waiting for an explanation.

"So what are you doing here Jason?" I asked, curious about his familiarity in my grandmother's house.

"I live here Mands!" came the shocking reply. "I have been since your parents passed away and Ma and Zoe needed help. In fact, I have been around since you decided to leave everyone in the lurch without so much as a call to let us know where you were or what happened to you. We were worried you know."

I felt a stab of guilt mixed with anger at his condescending tone. The nod of agreement from Ma and Zoe made my heart despair.

"I thought you would be too busy to worry, what with getting engaged to Lola!" I retorted, the heat returning to my body.

"If you would have stuck around long enough, you would have known that Lola was only out to trap me for my family's money. The only reason I got engaged to her was because she said she was pregnant!" he replied. Brown eyes sparkled with anger.

"Maybe you two need to talk in private," retorted Ma, slowly getting up and coming towards Zachary.

Zach squealed at her approach and grabbed my shoulder. "Mummy let's go home now please!" he said, climbing into my lap as Ma tried to reach out to cuddle him.

This was my chance to escape. Quickly, I stood up, pulling Zach tightly against my hip.

"Sorry Ma, we have to get back now. I have some work to do and we don't have long before we have to return home. Maybe I can come back another time and we can visit the cemetery together?"

Three pairs of eyes watched my agitated move to the front door. Sullen looks passed each face in turn and Ma made a move to follow me out, but Jason got up and gently put a restraining hand on her shoulder.

"Don't worry Ma. I'll walk her out." He came towards us and I could see Zachary's features playing in his father's face. He smiled reassuringly at me and gently put a hand under my elbow to politely guide me out the door.

"Bye Ma! I'll give you a call. By Zoe!" I called as I was led out into the lovely warm sunlight. Roses in bright reds and pinks grazed against my skirt and Zachary's legs, sending a nostalgic rush of happy childhood memories of running up and down this very path. Stones crunched underfoot as we crossed the driveway to the parked Corolla. Zachary was safely despatched into his seat, the seat belt wrapped around his skinny little body. It was strange not having to use a car seat for him. Once the door was closed, Jason followed me to the driver's side.

Strong hands pulled me against a solid chest. The musky scent of sweat and cologne filled my nose and panic threatened to choke me.

"Mandy, I missed you so much! You don't know what I've been through all these years, waiting for you. Do you realise I thought something bad had happened to you? Do you?" he said, kissing my eyes, my cheeks and my lips. His hands were heavy and held me in place, leaving no room to escape the amorous onslaught.

My hands automatically raised and pushed against his solid chest, feeling the sinewy muscle flex as his hand flew up to cover mine, trapping me even tighter against him. My mouth was covered by a savage kiss, deepening as I struggled to break free. Panting, he released me, watching my confusion and outrage. How dare he think it acceptable to just kiss me?

"Stop! Stop it!" I gasped at last. "What the hell do you think you're doing? You left me remember? What are you playing at looking after my family and living with them? What's your game?" I sputtered, anger choking my words.

"I had to do something to help them Mandy. You weren't here after the accident. Your father was going to lose his business because of the fire and I had to step in to help. I had the money to keep him afloat. So I became his partner and after he died, I have been running the business for Zoe and Ma."

"And Lola!" I added desperately trying to get my hands back from his chest.

"No! I told you. Lola and I are over! We have been for a long time. I've been waiting for you. I knew you would return someday and I had to see you to make things right. I still love you Mandy, no matter what happened in the past. Now that you're back, I won't let you go again!"

A dark choking feeling enveloped me as I looked deeply into the golden brown eyes filled with hope and passion. Was this what I had been waiting for? The father of my child willing to take back the years between us and start afresh? But he didn't know yet. He didn't know he was Zachary's father.

Alex Edwards was not a man who took chances. All his life he had played by the rules and prided himself on working hard, achieving whatever he set out to do and making a huge success out his life. Unfortunately, fate had other ideas about his happiness.

Growing up in an affluent family in the beautiful suburbs of Pretoria, South Africa, Alex received his education from the top private school in the area and further education at Rhodes University. At the age of twenty-three, he was offered a position with a prestigious law firm in Johannesburg. There he met his future wife, Sienna, who was an undergraduate volunteering at the firm. It was love at first sight and within months, they had announced their engagement. Sienna had been brought up in South Africa, but was originally from Harare, Zimbabwe. Her family were well established in the Borrowdale area and Sienna had been taught from a young age that hard work achieved results. With a sweet temperament, strong attitude and startling good looks, she won the heart of the most promising young Practising Attorney at Willow and Brooks. Their families celebrated the match, welcoming the couple with open arms.

The newlywed couple settled down in Zimbabwe, choosing to live closer to Sienna's family in Borrowdale. They knew it would not be forever, but with Alex working long hours and taking frequent trips out of the country, it made sense for her to be situated closer to family and friends.

Sienna was an avid jogger and loved to run in the early morning coolness before the heat of the day made it unbearable to pound the streets in her Nike trainers. The twist of fate happened one fateful morning in early May. Alex was taking a trip to the United States, assisting in the acquisition of some properties in Florida. His flight was due to take off early in the morning and Sienna decided to forfeit her run to see him off. After a passionate morning of heady embraces and loving kisses, Alex tore off to the airport, late for his flight but with a big smile on his face. He loved his wife so much. She made him feel strong and vibrant. With a silly grin, he checked in and sat in the Executive Lounge, reminiscing over their morning lovemaking. His return wouldn't come soon enough. Unfortunately, Alex didn't know it would be the last time he saw Sienna alive.

The news only reached him a day later. They could not identify her body and only after tracing her jogging pattern from witnesses who saw her every morning, they concluded it was Sienna Edwards. Alex's flight home was the longest, most heart breaking trip he had ever made. The world around him had shattered into a million pieces. As a man who had always played by the rules and followed some semblance of order, everything was jarred; a kaleidoscope of the life he had imagined.

He quit his job and opened up an investment company. By increasing travel to different countries offering opportunities to develop his property portfolio, he managed to work seven days a week, never taking personal holidays or breaks. It blanked out life's normality; a chance to sit and have a cup of coffee in the morning in his own home. Anything to cancel a normal life and the intimate promises of happiness it once held.

His dogged perseverance and hard worked paid off and within two years of Sienna's untimely death, his company had established a reputation for professionalism and ingenuity across the globe. For Alex, the money meant nothing more than keeping him fed and watered. The aching within could be subdued by the burial of mind and soul in month long negotiations and travelling that left him wondering which country he would wake up in next. Sienna's spirit kept vigil in the back of his mind, a constant reminder of his loneliness late at night when the quiet made an inescapable path to memories he desperately tried to bury.

That is, until his company agreed to lead an investigation into properties held in Zimbabwe. His policy was to work alone whenever possible and this assignment threw a spanner in the works. He had provisionally agreed to some assistance from Alann & Cook, but never imagined it would come in the form of the most beautiful, somewhat scatty woman he had ever laid his eyes upon. Sienna's warm memory felt deluged with cold, hard hands in comparison to the brown haired beauty before him. Guilty pain swallowed his heart and sent an electric surge through his body at the memory of what was lost.

Alex felt a physical reaction to being near Amanda, something he had not expected to feel every again. Her emerald green eyes sparkled with pools of mischief, even when she tried to hide her true feelings, and a sense of vulnerability hung around her, making him want to envelope her into his warm embrace and keep her safe from the world.

Zachary was a surprise that took him totally off balance. Though he was no celibate, Alex had made sure that any relations he had to satisfy his libido were with single women without children. He had never met a child that pulled at his heart with such a direct impact at first meeting. No matter how much he tried keeping his emotions in check, the brown eyed little imp had him wrapped around his little finger and had managed to hang onto his heart strings as though he were his own child!

The combination of Amanda's silence over bringing Zachary on a business trip and her passionate hot and cold attitude kept him intrigued. What was she hiding that made her move back when other women would have crawled into bed with him at the first opportunity? He had met his fair share of gold diggers, and one with a child should have been keen at his show of interest. Instead, emerald eyes showed fear each time he showed any advance towards her. Alex knew more of her history than he let on, but he wanted to give her a chance to open up to him.

———————————————

The sound of tyres crunching on stones made Alex sit up and peer through the dining room window. Amanda and Zachary were returning from their shopping trip. The car moved slowly and he could make out her face through the windshield. She looked upset and slightly dishevelled. His heart lurched with worry, a foreign feeling to him. Why did he feel so responsible for her and want to run out the door to find out what happened to make her look that way? Without a second though at the answer, he was out of the chair and through the kitchen to meet the car at the back of the house.

The fiery orange ball in the sky was slowly disappearing behind the tall eucalyptus trees and they swayed in unison as the wind played with their long fluttering leaves, making them sigh with delight. As she emerged from the car, the golden highlights in her long wavy hair lit with fiery colour in the dying embers of the day. He stopped in his tracks, admiring the natural beauty that she unconsciously possessed. Long shapely legs peeked out from under her denim skirt and the soft white blouse she wore caught her curves and made him want to peel off each layer to reveal what was hidden beneath. She looked up at him. Streaks of tears shed earlier marked her cheeks and smudged eyes. He covered the distance between them and took her in his arms, holding her gently.

"What happened? Did someone attack you? Are you okay?" Fury filled his chest.

"Yes. Yes. I ... I just ..." she hiccupped, trying to hold back more tears. "I need to get Zach out of the car. He's fallen asleep."

As soft as a whisper, she slipped out of his arms and went around the car to retrieve her son. Her son, not his. He could sense there was something going on and she had lied about going to the shops. Was it her family that had caused her such concern? He would have to find out but first, she looked like she needed a stiff drink and help with Zachary.

"So, do you feel like talking now?" Alex asked, putting his wine glass down next to his half empty plate.

Dinner had been a quiet affair with the two of them eating a warmed up curry they found in the fridge provided by the kind Mrs Ismail. Amanda's plate looked pretty much the same as when she started the meal, though her wine glass had been refilled at least twice. Her eyes were like soft green velvet and her relaxed expression allowed the pronounced pout of her bottom lip to naturally stick out. She unconsciously teased it with her teeth.

"As you've guessed, I've been frolicking about this afternoon" she giggled, showing just how inebriated she was. She gave another laugh and blinked at Alex from under half closed eyes. "Do you want to know where I've been?" Her eyes darkened and a slight flush covered her skin. "I've been to see my family. A family I left behind a long time ago. And you know what? I missed them so, so much!"

Alex frowned, watching her slip into an alcoholic stupor. This woman had no control after a few glasses of wine. She was slowly slipping out of her seat whilst gesturing to the air and he quickly got up and reached her before she toppled right out of her seat. With a heave she was up in his arms, her body draped across his chest. Soft trusting eyes looked up at him with such great sadness in their green depths that he felt like he was drowning in his own sorrow, matching his pain with hers. An urge to quench the hunger and squash the pain overcame him.

He lowered his mouth onto hers, tasting the wine and the warm of her breath. Plunging deeper with his tongue, he heard her groan with awareness and his own body tightened in response. Gently lifting her closer to him he traced a path of kisses from her mouth down to her throat. It was all he could do to control himself and not to take her right there, tearing off the light shirt dress she had changed into before dinner.

Amanda's eyes opened and the sadness was gone, replaced by a similar hunger he felt deep within his body. A huntress lurked under the pain and her green eyes mimicked cat's eyes, glinting with unashamed passion.

"I want you Alex. Just for tonight, I would like to forget that I'm so alone." Her golden cheeks glowed from the alcohol and though he could make out a slight slur in her speech, her eyes held him with their intensity.

Alex's arms were straining and he wanted the freedom to explore her body with more than just his mouth. Shifting her weight he turned and carried her down the passageway to the bedrooms, stopping outside his bedroom door to look down at her one last time. He felt the guilt of his dead wife weighing down on his chest and tried to block it out. The face of this beautiful woman in front of him held the guilt at bay and his sexual hunger cried out to be satisfied. They shared a look that answered the unspoken question of consent and with that, the door to Alex's room closed behind them, opening a night of passion that both of them craved.

CHAPTER EIGHT

"Mummy! Mummy! Where are you?" a tiny voice called from a distance. "Mum! I need you!"

I opened my eyes and could see that it was already bright and warm outside. Where am I? It took a while to take in the surroundings with the pounding headache and cat-shat-on-your-tongue feeling in my mouth. Oh no! Zachary! Was that him calling me?

I tried to get up quickly but my head and body refused to oblige, body parts aching as though they had not been used in a long time, which induced a total recollection of the night before.

A second voice could be heard from further in the house; a voice calling Zach to breakfast. A man's voice! I took in my surroundings again. The dark furnishings and rather large bed, clothes strewn across the floor and of course, catching a glimpse of my reflection in the mirror, a stark naked woman with crazy sex hair and glowing eyes staring back at her. Oh crap! I carefully gathered the sheet around me and made my way across the room, stopping to pick up the guilty dress and underwear staring back at me. I opened the door ever so slightly to check if the coast was clear I quickly tiptoed into the bathroom across the passageway. There was no way I was going to use Alex's bathroom and get caught in there. It was bad enough I had overslept and now

Zachary was looking for me. What sort of mother had I become?

It took a good half hour to shower, change and try to kill the hangover banging in my head so that I could show my face to the rest of the people in the house. As I walked down the passageway to the kitchen I could hear the voices of Zach and Alex in the lounge, happily playing with the Thomas train set the Ismail's had left for him. There was a deeper voice singing and humming outside and I could make out Sonzo weeding the front garden; his hat perched slightly askew on his balding head and his weathered hands working furiously amongst the ferns and Busy Lizzies. I peered around the door to watch Alex's dark head close to Zach's, the two of them so deep into their game they did not notice me watching them. It pulled at my heart to think that they were forming a strong bond. Jason would find out soon about Zachary and then what would he do, knowing that I had run off with his child?

After grabbing a muffin and a fresh cup of coffee, I felt brave enough to face the boys and greeted them cheerfully. Alex looked up at me with hooded eyes, his expression friendly but guarded. Zach gave me a big hug and gabbled on about how he had had breakfast with Alex and was telling him all about Grandma, Zoe and Jason. Oh no! I blanched. Looking at Alex I could see that he had a grim expression on his face. How much had Zachary shared about our first family visit yesterday? The bite of muffin in my mouth seemed harder to swallow and the coffee didn't help it down, but the fear of being discovered held it tightly in my throat.

"Please excuse me, I've got something stuck in my throat," I managed to croak before scuttling back to the kitchen. Through blurred vision, I tried to fill a glass with water from the tap when strong warm hands took the glass from me.

"Here, drink this" Alex instructed. "When you're done choking on your food, would you like to explain to me exactly what you are playing at?"

I gulped and wiped the tears from my eyes. "What do you mean?" I asked, hoping he would elaborate.

"Don't play games Amanda. You slept with me last night. You asked me to and now I find out that you had hooked up with your ex yesterday. What am I, some sort of fall guy for your broken relationship?!

"How dare you say I asked you? You knew I had too much to drink and took advantage. I didn't know what I was doing."

"Don't you dare say I took advantage of you? You knew exactly what you were doing and we were both consenting adults. Look, if you are in a relationship, just be honest with me. No games!" he glowered at me, anger palpable just below the calm surface.

"No I am not in the habit of playing games and yes I did meet my ex-boyfriend, but there is nothing there. Now if you are quite finished with the third degree I would like to get back to my son."

Alex stared at me for a few more seconds then took a step back, shaking his head and running his hands through his hair.

"I should have known you would be trouble. And thanks for the heads up that you have more than just distant family in this godforsaken country!" With that, he stalked out of the kitchen and disappeared into another part of the house.

Shaken by the encounter I returned to the lounge to play with Zach. The feeling of panic rose in me and I knew trouble was lurking around the corner. Alex now knew that I came from this country. It was only a matter of time before he found out about my history. Maybe it was time to disappear for a while until things cooled down. The only place to go would be back to Ma's house. At least there I could be with my family ... and Zachary's father.

Alex was holed up in the dining room on the phone when I left the house and made my way back to Belvedere. I wondered if I should have called first, but thought the surprise of my return would be welcomed. The gate was wide open and I drove straight up the drive to the house. Ma was outside in the garden, pruning the roses and instructing Kumbi what to do in the garden for the next week.

Zachary seemed to warm up to his great grandmother on the second meeting and even gave her a hug to go with his greeting. Ma was happy and I relaxed a little, feeling my old self return. Being here, in these warm familiar surroundings made me feel young and free again, as though all the troubles of my past were slowly vanishing. And then I spotted Zoe staring at us from her bedroom window. Her unsmiling face and the hatred that shone in her eyes frightened me. She seemed fixated on Zachary and did not notice me watching her. Slowly her eyes lifted to me when Zach came towards me and she shook herself, pasting a fake smile on her gruesome face and waving. A cold shiver ran down my spine. I needed to make amends and somehow bridge the gap between us.

When she came out to join us, I hugged her tight, telling her how much I missed her again. She merely stood there and smiled once I let her go. It was going to be an upward struggle trying to get my Zoe back. Zach grabbed her hand and dragged her skinny jean clad body around the garden, questioning her on all the different flowers and smells. He was in his element outside and loved the fruit that could be picked straight from the trees, happily sitting on Zo Zo's lap (as he was instructed to call her) eating a plum. Zoe seemed to soften around him and I caught her stroking his hair and gently hugging him to her every once in a while. Ma was pleased with her progress and when we were further away from the two, she explained what Zoe had been like over the past few years.

"When Zo recovered from the accident and came out of the hospital, she refused to be amongst people and would stay in her room for days. Your father was so distraught, he let her get away with it, but your mother wanted her to face reality and become strong. She hadn't said a word for months and the doctors couldn't find anything wrong with her. It caused them to fight so much in the house. I was allowed to visit again, since you were not around to buffer the fighting. Eish Ma, it was hard! So much pain and hurt and then they find out that the business is doomed. I tell you Mands, if Jason had not stepped in, we would have lost everything…everything Ma!"

"What about the insurance? Surely it would have paid out once they found out I wasn't responsible for the fire and it was an accident" I asked, feeling a strange liberation being able to talk about the past.

Ya, well Ma, they still questioned why you ran away. I mean Mands, seriously, what were you thinking running away instead of saving your sister, huh?" she asked, hands sitting furiously on her hips.

"Ma, I swear to you I didn't start that fire. I was called to the warehouse by an anonymous phone call. The person's voice sounded husky and strange, and I was instructed to go to the warehouse if I wanted to save Dad. I thought Dad was in trouble and went straight there. When I got upstairs to the offices, something or someone knocked me out. The building was burning around me when I woke up. The phone lines weren't working so my safest bet was to run for help. The building was supposed to be empty. Dad was the only one who worked in the warehouse over the weekends, so there was no reason to search for her. She was supposed to be staying the week at Penelope's house."

"But when you ran the police were already on their way. Someone had called for help and that's why you were spotted running from the building," replied Ma, scratching a balding spot behind her ear. "Do you think that someone was trying to hurt you as well as your sister?"

"I don't know, but I'm going to have to find out."

"Maybe Jason knows. I'll ask him when he gets home. He still goes to have Sunday lunch with his own family.

His mum is not well you know. You should go visit them and say hi since you're here."

Ma gave me a strange look and I pretended not to notice. I didn't want to spend any more time with him or his family than I had to. It was confusing enough thinking about our last meeting and how that had ended. I also remembered how much Jason's mother disliked me, thinking I was a bad influence on her son because of my free and easy ways. Her grim face lingered in my mind and I shivered at the thought of having to be in her company again.

"Okay I'll see if there's enough time later Ma," was my half-hearted response. Thank goodness she left it at that and we went in to enjoy a delicious lunch ourselves. I watched Zoe communicate with Zach through hand gestures and smiles. She seemed content in herself but I worried if there was another reason why she didn't speak.

Ma accepted her silence and didn't bother addressing the subject again. There were so many questions I wanted to ask about Zoe's injuries. What was she doing at the warehouse in the first place? Who paid for the medical expenses if the business was failing? Why didn't they send Zoe to a specialist to find out why she couldn't speak anymore? I had to get to the bottom of it, but gently. No-one wanted to answer my questions. Instead, they had more pressing questions for me and as much as

I tried to answer them, they refused to believe me! Trust was the missing element in my family and I think I was to blame for it.

The cemetery off Pioneer Street stood close to an area called Magaba. It was a slum of sorts, filled with African people who had drifted off their farms and rural plots of land to make it in the city. Most had to resort to a life of crime to make a living and others worked hard for the little they were paid, sending most of their earnings back home to feed their starving families. A certain area of Magaba sold anything you needed to repair your house, car, boat or even an aeroplane!

The problem was that when you parked in the area, whilst you were conducting business with the not-so-friendly entrepreneurs, their partners would be stripping your car and probably selling the parts back to you without you knowing! It made for interesting business transactions. Only the brave ventured to that part of town to do business.

I stood at the foot of my parents' grave in the hot afternoon sun. Tombstones lay toppled where vandals had tried to carry them away to resell the slate and granite blocks. The ground was unkempt with tufts of grass sprouting out from the cracked walkways in between the graves. The six foot wall surrounding the cemetery grounds had crumbled holes where eyes avidly watched for a chance to rob the unwary mourners.

The car had to be locked properly in case those watching eyes decided to make a move whilst the family prayed at the graveside. Mum and Dad's resting place looked out of place with its tidy grave and a fresh vase of flowers stood next to the semi upright stone. It was a beautiful dark grey granite stone with scripted writing giving information on the dates and an inscription saying, "Gone but not forgotten".

My knees ached as I knelt and silently prayed for forgiveness. The hot wind played havoc with my curls and the sound of the traffic permeated the silence of the graveyard. After a few minutes, Zachary moaned that he wanted to go home. Ma and Zoe watched me stand and stretch, before leading our little party of four back to the parked car.

The eyes at the wall watched in fascination as we departed. They probably descended on the grave to see what lovely knick-knacks were left for their choice pickings before the car had turned the corner and left the cemetery. Life was hard and even if the flowers could be sold; it meant a meal for one in a town where everyone scrambled to survive.

The car was silent and each person seemed lost in their own thoughts as we drove back to the house. It felt as though our family was slowly coming back together. At least I hoped in my heart of hearts that it could happen. Was I being naïve again? Probably. I would have to wait and see.

CHAPTER NINE

Alex controlled his anger and focused on the tasks ahead. It was time to do more than just a light background check on Amanda Glenson. He never took risks when working with strangers and she was no exception.

He already knew about the Glenson family and had read the newspaper reports on their family business going down after a fire, but Zachary had been kind enough to fill in a few more details that started to move jigsaw pieces into place. Alex wanted to kick himself for coming so close to falling for a woman he had only known for less than a few weeks. So what if she made him forget his past and actually imagine a happy future? He had been alone for so long, what difference did it make how she felt in his arms and the senses she awakened when she smiled at him? He had to focus and get the business done so that he could return to his normal life. Alone.

He spent the rest of Sunday making calls and calling in favours to find out the full history of this elusive woman that was staying with him. David Gallia, an old school friend from South Africa who had moved to Zimbabwe many years before now worked within the Zimbabwe Police Force as a Detective Inspector and was able to furnish him with the report on the fire. It was sad to see that Amanda's sister was injured in the fire, but more surprising was the report of a suspect seen running from the building and the consequential arrest of Amanda as the culprit. There were missing pages from the report and David seemed to think that someone might have tampered with the file to help Amanda escape a custodial sentence. Alex poured over the faxed documents and tried to decipher the evidence laid out against her. He could not imagine Amanda being involved in such a horrendous crime. Surely there was a reason for her being there and why didn't she save her own sister? Maybe the missing papers included her statement. He had a lot of questions that needed answering but he knew he couldn't approach her directly. She obviously had something to hide and if he spooked her, she might run again as she had five years before, with her baby.

It was dusk before he moved from the computer to take a break. Stretching out his stiff, aching frame, he looked around and noticed the house was in darkness. Amanda must have left earlier without his noticing. It seemed so empty and lifeless without her voice or Zach's constant conversation and laughter. A little ache filled his chest which he automatically rubbed away without thinking. It wasn't going to do him any good to form attachments with this crazy family.

Shaking his head, he turned back to the phone and called a taxi to take him into the city. It was time to find out what the night life looked like in Harare. No time like the present to wash away the emerald green eyes haunting his every waking hour.

The next few days became a whirl of action and meetings, trying to substantiate the business they had been sent to accomplish in the first place. The Partels were a very affluent family in Harare and owned more than one property. Most were residential houses with a few commercial properties let out to smaller businesses. Finding the tenancy agreements and sending out notices of termination was the simple part. The difficulty came in removing the tenants who had relatives in the political pool and refused to leave or even take notice of the letters, threatening to take the properties for themselves. It would be a battle in the court to decide who had a right to the properties in the end. With Mr Ismail's help, the letters were sent out and appropriate court dates set for tenants fighting removal, thereby leaving the commercial properties for Alex and Amanda to settle.

Working together was not easy. Underlying currents of distrust could be felt and Alex was aloof and condescending in his treatment towards her. It was his only protection against her sultry eyes and undeniably attractive body. Amanda felt the shame of lying to Alex and kept her distance from his disdain. The faster they completed the business, the faster she could book the tickets to go back to her beautiful little house in England. It was wonderful spending time with her family, but she knew the hidden accusations they kept at bay. Amanda could feel the distrust from Zoe and Ma, no matter how many times she apologised and tried to explain her defence.

There was nothing more she could do. She kept her professional head and managed to expedite the closure of two properties without Alex's help. He hired his own car to expedite matters and by the end of the week, they had visited all the properties around the Harare Central Business District and sent out letters of notice of termination of tenancy. One of the commercial properties was located in an upcoming industrial business area called Graniteside. It was a very dusty place with new complexes being constructed around the site. Dry clay sand blew across new roads and coated the warehouses in a grey dusting. Both Alex and Amanda attended a meeting with the tenant of 15 Graniteside Road to find out if he would be willing to buy the property he was renting out from the Partel family.

Mr Seke was a timid man who had built his own furniture business from the back of his house in Mbare. His success allowed the business to move into a large warehouse where the assembly of handmade lounge suites in magnificent colours and materials could be made to order. He had at least 10 workers on staff and seemed enthusiastic at the idea of holding the property rights to the warehouse and land. Amanda had prepared the deeds to highlight the price and terms of sale, which he agreed to without hesitation.

It made for a pleasant meeting and they ended it with a business lunch at the local restaurant which serviced the workers in the area. Alex and Amanda had taken separate cars to the meeting as previous appointments had taken them to odd ends of town earlier in the morning. Arriving and parking at the restaurant, they congregated outside the restaurant doors in the stifling, dry heat. Suddenly, someone called out Amanda's name. A large burly shape pushed through the lunch crowd towards them, a hand waving to catch Amanda's attention. It was Jason.

"Hi Bumblebee!" he greeted as he approached the group and gave her a quick hug. She shyly returned the hug and stepped back to see Alex giving Jason a hooded glare. Jason quickly introduced himself to everyone in the group and was invited to join them by Mr Seke who seemed to have done business with Jason on previous occasions. Their amicable chatter covered the awkwardness Amanda felt and Alex's searing stares at her ex-boyfriend.

Once seated and the orders for food placed, the conversation drifted to business and social topics. Alex decided to take the opportunity to find out more about Amanda's ex and what better way than fish out exactly what he did. Jason remained calm through the interrogation and his brown eyes flickered with amusement as he watched Alex try to break through the barriers and ruffle his feathers. During a break in the conversation, Jason whispered to Amanda, "Is this your boss or your boyfriend because he is seriously giving me beans for nothing here?"

Amanda shrugged her shoulders and continued sipping the cool sparkling water she had ordered with her meal. Mr Seke interjected and guided the conversation back to business, for which she was grateful. After a gruelling hour of watching Alex and Jason stare each other down at every opportunity, she offered to take Mr Seke back to his offices and turned to inform Alex that she would be picking Zach up from school and then would start the applications for the transfer of deeds. He nodded at her, barely acknowledging her words. Jason got up from the table, saying he also had to get back to work and bent to give Amanda a kiss on her cheek. He smiled wickedly and said, "I'll see you soon Bumblebee and we'll catch up from where we left off!" With that, he smiled at the two men at the table and walked out the door, disappearing into the glare of the afternoon sun.

Alex's mood seemed to shift to a darker place, as he threw his napkin on the table, forcibly pushing his chair back, attracting the attention of the other patrons. Both Amanda and Mr Seke looked up at him in surprise. "Sorry, I have some urgent work to do as well. Mr Seke, it was a pleasure meeting you and of course we will have the paperwork filed as soon as possible for a smooth transition."

Shaking his hand, he smiled slightly and turned his attention to Amanda. "That is, if Ms Glenson can keep her mind on the job!" With that he left the table and stalked out of the restaurant. Both Amanda and Mr Seke were left at the table in an awkward silence.

"My dear girl, I think you had better be careful with those two men," retorted Mr Seke. "They are like bulls, and if you do not choose your favourite soon, both will fight until one is no more."

Amanda smiled in embarrassment and nodded in agreement. There was nothing she could add to that. As soon as she had dropped him off at his Graniteside offices and fetched Zach from school, she drove back to the house. The gate was open and Alex stood waiting for them to park. Once the car had stopped, Zach pushed his door open and ran to give Alex a big hug. His bare skinny arms wrapped themselves lovingly around Alex's neck, the khaki shirt and shorts he wore as the uniform crumpling in his haste. He had loved his school from the start and had settled in really well. Belvedere School was not the closest to Avondale, but it was the same school that Amanda had attended and she was secretly pleased that her son could enjoy the same memories she had as a child.

His favourite part of the day was seeing Alex wait for him to come home and telling him all about his day and the friends he had made. Alex happily lifted him into his arms and took him inside, asking appropriate questions to accompany Zach's unstoppable news. Amanda walked in on her own, pondering over her relationship with this moody man.

Evening came and Zach was safely tucked up in bed. Amanda had been working on the title deeds and mortgage documents all evening and had only stopped to bath Zachary and read him a bedtime story. When she returned to the office/dining room, she found Alex waiting for her with a glass of wine. He smiled in encouragement when she stopped at the door and just stared at him warily.

"I don't want to fight Mandy," was his simple answer to her body language. He came forward, handing her the glass and moved back to take a seat on one of the dining chairs. She followed and sighed as she sat down, exhausted after a long day of meetings and paperwork. He watched her as she rolled her shoulders up and down.

"Tired?" he asked, standing up and moving behind her chair to give her shoulders a massage. "It was a long day today but we have accomplished most of what we have set out to do. We should be able to get back to the UK before the end of the month," he continued without waiting for an answer.

She froze slightly at the touch of his warm hands on her tired shoulders. It was a little piece of heaven feeling the warmth from his strong fingers seep through as he stroked the aches out of her tense shoulders but she didn't want to fall into a trap. It took all her will power not to sigh out loud and melt into his arms. He stopped and looked down at her head covered in long waves of golden brown hair. Without thinking, he picked up a lock of her hair and rubbed it, feeling the soft texture, then gently let it fall back with the other locks cascading down her back. She kept still and didn't turn around. He covered her shoulders again with his hands and pushed her slightly back so that he could catch a glimpse of the expression on her face.

She looked up at him and could see the sparks lighting the darkness in his coal eyes. Slowly, he lowered his face to hers and kissed her until her resistance melted under the onslaught of gentleness. She sighed and responded. He slowly came round to stand in front of her, kissing her until she was breathless.

Heat welled up around them and Amanda reached up to stroke his hair, running her cool fingers through the unruly waves of darkness and pressing him closer to deepen the kiss. Her eyes were still closed when she felt his hands release her and he stepped back out of her embrace, leaving a cold emptiness behind him. She opened her eyes to find him watching her and the passion that had been there a minute ago was replaced with cold hard stone.

"You'd better get some sleep before you claim I took advantage of you when you were tired," he said and abruptly left the room.

She sat there for a few more minutes trying to digest what had just happened. There was no mistaking the fire that burned through both of them when they were together, but he obviously did not trust her and she felt that she couldn't trust herself.

With a lump in her throat she switched off everything and decided to go to bed to nurse her injured pride. Tomorrow was another day and now it was a countdown to going back to her peaceful and calm life in England. She just had to endure a few more weeks then all this would be in the past.

CHAPTER TEN

Chapped lips smiled up at the tall, squared off man standing next to the slim, athletic woman who seemed at odds with herself. They were standing in front of a dusty Toyota corolla in the middle of a sandy road leading out to the National Parks close to Lake Chivero (known previously as Lake Mcilwaine).

Zach looked up again at the man and woman next to him and thought how wonderful it was to have a family. Alex was like the dad he never knew but had imagined a million times in his little mind. Though he was five years old, he understood that his life was not the same as those of his friends in England. They were in a foreign country that his mother claimed to be her home and the man standing next to her was her protector and someone she cared deeply about, but never said it.

Zach was lifted into the air and placed on Alex's shoulders. He was thrilled and frightened at the same time. The big blue dome above his head couldn't be more different to what he was used to. The sky seemed to radiate warmth and happiness and made him think of his many walks to school in the cold greyness his childhood only knew.

The sun shone down on his head and he could feel the heat pressing into his skin, burning him a golden brown. His lips hurt and a water bottle was pressed into his small hands from which he drank deeply. The sweet taste of clean, fresh water moistened his dry lips and he smiled at his mother with appreciation. It was the perfect day in this hot place and they were going to see elephants, and giraffes, and rhinos, and many other animals that he had as plastic toys. His mind was spinning with excitement.

The tall dark-skinned man in front of them was talking in a strange sing-song accent and explained the rules of visiting the national parks. They were not allowed walking around by themselves and they had to stay in the car at all times in case a lion came to eat them. Startling white teeth revealed themselves as he peeled back his lips in a huge grin. He giggled like a girl. Zach could feel the laughter bubbling inside of him and let it out. No-one frowned at him for bad behaviour. Instead, everyone joined in the laughter and yes, it was the best day ever!

Suddenly the talking stopped and it was time to get back into the car and continue travelling along the bumpy, dusty road. He sat back on the large back seat with the seat belt wrapped around him and smiled, joy bursting out of him. After a few minutes into the journey, they spotted two tall giraffes elegantly walking amongst some rather large flat-topped trees. They stripped the leaves with their big blue tongues and twisted them into their gaping mouths.

Zach pointed to the giant deer that ran past with huge antlers. Mum laughed and said they were Impala. They jumped so high and ran away when the car made a noise. Zebra ran together and short fat pigs with horns darted back into the bushes or the long dry grass that seemed to surround everything.

What felt like forever to the five year old was a short journey to the adults, and soon they arrived at a chalet they had booked in the middle of the park. The building was nondescript and did not call out comfort, but the barbeque set up outside and the quiet lake only a few metres away made the place look like heaven. With the car parked and strict instructions not to go too close to the water, Zach walked around exploring the area for bugs and smaller wildlife scuttling in the bushes and rocks. Dirt covered everything, the dry tufts of grass sharp as he separated the long blades to find another fat grasshopper.

Alex and Amanda unloaded the car, laughing and teasing each other with a freedom they hadn't felt in the past week. They had decided that after their initial onslaught of work, a little downtime over the weekend wouldn't hurt anyone and had booked a chalet in the National Parks on the outskirts of Harare to take in the natural beauty on offer.

Once the unpacking was done and the insect repellent sprayed in gallons to remove the cockroaches, spiders and mosquitoes in the chalet, Alex and Amanda walked back out into the burning midday heat. They found Zach crouched low, watching a dung beetle make its slow progress across a dusty pathway. He was so enrapt in the beetle's progress that he didn't hear them approach, and they decided to leave him whilst they took a walk to the end of a pier jutting out into the silent lake.

Birds called out noisily to each other and buzzing bees rasped past in the wildflowers decorating the banks of the lake. A fish made a splash and plonked back into the water, causing ripples which expanded outwards.

"I want you to know that if you are in trouble, or need to talk to me, I'm listening Mandy," Alex said, watching the gentle glide of a hawk in the distance. "I can't play games with you and I know that you have a past you don't want to share with me. But, I would rather be honest with you and let you know that if you need me, I'm there." His muscle in his cheek flickered as he bit down hard.

Amanda watched the hawk and sighed. It would be lovely to tell him everything and let him carry part of the burden of her past, but what if he thought she was to blame and informed her work that she was a fugitive from a crime committed years ago. He had the power to destroy her family and her life in England.

"Thank you Alex. My family have been here for a long time and yes I grew up in this place. But there is nothing to tell other than bad family reunions and past mistakes. I'm sure you have your own share of mistakes made that you don't want to discuss with anyone?" She braved a glance at his serious face and watched for a reaction. He turned to her and took in her expression. His eyes darkened and the flicker in his jaw appeared again. "Yes, I suppose we all have a history or past that shouldn't be shared."

With a sigh he turned back to the breath-taking view of the lake in front of him. "Let's just enjoy this weekend and each other. No holds barred. What do you think?" He turned back to her, a smile lighting his face and eyes, making him roguishly handsome. She nodded and giggled, feeling the weight of the moment lift off her shoulders. They could have made a perfect couple; they knew how to break past issues and move forward, if they had a chance.

Without hesitation he picked her up and ran to the edge of the pier, jumping his full length into the lake and taking her screaming and protesting with him. Zach looked up from his beetle, eyes bright with interest. His heart leaped with joy at the sound of his mother laughing and squealing with delight as she splashed about, trying to dunk Alex under the glassy depths of the lake. He stood up and ran to the pier, not thinking of anything other than how happy he was and jumped in. Two pairs of hands caught him and laughter surrounded him as the warm wetness seeped through his sandals and clothes.

That night, as they sat around the fire having eaten their fill of barbequed meat, and watched the stars twinkling so brightly above their heads, Zach secretly wished that this life would never end and he prayed that Alex would never leave them. He squeezed his eyes tightly shut and made the wish. Alex felt him stiffen in his arms and, thinking he was cold, wrapped a blanket around him. He gave him a tight hug. That was how Zach fell asleep that night and little did he know that the warmth of that memory would stay with him for the rest of his life.

The thunder rumbled across the grey sky and lightning flared, sparking off buildings and trees in the distance. The November air felt heavy with the coming storm and an eerie silence filled a usually noisy day.

"Are you sure you don't mind looking after Zach for me Ma?" I asked for the hundredth time.

She nodded as though understanding my reluctance to leave him.

"Don't worry my girl. Go have a good time and you'll see him when you get back, happy as anything!" She smiled and pushed me towards the door. "Go now before he misses you and makes a fuss. Zoe will keep him occupied. Oh and Mandy…have fun okay?"

I heard tyres crunching on stones outside and knew that my date had arrived. My heart fluttered and I wanted to run back into the house and grab Zachary to me as a safety net. Well, fortune favours the brave and I had to be extremely brave for my mission tonight. The car hooted, and Ma gave me a quick kiss and another shove. I smiled back and ran out into the cloudy twilight.

As soon as I got into the car, a pair of hands found my face and I was drawn into a long, languid kiss that was wet and overpowering. Jason released me and smiled. He had asked me out several times before but I had refused. I knew I would have to meet him and tell him about Zachary. Hence the date tonight. He was dressed in a dark blue shirt with grey trousers that clenched around his strong thighs and the shirt stretched against his rigid chest as he released my face.

"Hey gorgeous! I'm so happy you agreed to come out with me at last. Let's go get some dinner and then maybe we can find a quiet place to reminisce over old times," he said, dimples showing in the semi darkness. I nodded, not trusting myself to speak yet.

We drove to a restaurant in the middle of the Harare Gardens. A quaint little place that served Italian food

111

and had the best pizza money could buy. We ordered our meals, refusing the starters and sat back to enjoy the ambiance of the place. Soft music lilted over our heads and the floral furniture gave a feeling of warmth and homeliness. I looked back at Jason to find him smiling and watching me.

"What?" I asked, feeling slightly uncomfortable.

"Nothing!" he grinned. "I just remember how much you hated it when I sat staring at you. You used to complain saying that you felt like a bug was stuck on your face or something like that. Do you remember?"

"Yes and I still hate it!"

"Well you look the same ... so beautiful. I missed you so much. I missed your laugh, your smiles and the way you always looked away when you were embarrassed by something. But most of all, I missed your friendship and the time we spent together, just talking," His eyes were bright with the happy memories of the past.

"If I recall, most of the time we spent together you were trying to get into my pants," was my caustic response.

"Well you can't blame a guy Bumblebee. I mean everyone I know used to want to be with you and I was the lucky one you chose! I guess I always thought that you had had so many other lovers and then to find out I was your first ... Wow! Well, I felt honoured Mands. I just want you to know that." His sincerity did not stop me from cringing and I looked around, hoping the other diners couldn't hear our conversation.

Thankfully the food arrived, ending the awkward conversation. I had learned my lesson with alcohol and ordered a soft drink to accompany my meal. My lasagne stared back at me, as I tried to find the strength to open my mouth and say what was needed. Jason wolfed down his delicious looking pizza as though there were rabid dogs chasing him, and only came up for air once his plate was clean. Grinning at me, he asked if I wanted my food, which I happily passed on to the human waste disposal unit.

Dessert was even faster in arriving and I was losing my nerve, trying to find a way to open the conversation on Zachary. The bill was paid and we decided to take a walk around the park surrounding the restaurant. The thunderstorm was still threatening and the heavy oppressed air gave us the feeling that we were the only people out in the middle of the darkness. Jason grabbed my hand and we walked in silence for a while, the scent of Night Queen and Jasmine surrounding us from the hedges. We came up to a bench and sat in unison, taking in the peacefulness of the evening. My nerves couldn't stand it any longer. It was now or never.

"Jason, there is something I have to tell you. You touched on it earlier this evening when you talked about our relationship." I gulped and tried to swallow the panic rising within my gut. "I ... I have a confession to make."

He stared at me, trying to make out my expression in the dim street lights.

"Whatever it is, you can tell me Bumblebee. You know that right?" he said, his sincere brown eyes giving me the same innocent stare Zach gave me every day.

"There is no easy way to tell you this ... Okay ... Zachary is your son. Our one time together ... well that was the result!" I pushed on. "I don't expect you to do anything or suddenly be his father, but I wanted you to know before I returned to England. If you would like to keep in touch with him, that's fine. But if you don't, well, that is fine too. I just needed to let you know." The air rushed out of my lungs and I sat looking at him, waiting for his response.

Jason stared at me as though I had grown an extra head. He shook his own head a couple of times and got up, pacing in front of me. Suddenly, he sat down again, grabbing my hands. I could feel his pulse racing through his rough calloused hands as they squeezed mine.

"All this time, you knew I had a son and didn't care to share the information? All this time that you've been here? How could you Amanda? How dare you?" He stood up again and paced some more. Turning to me his hands shoved deep into his pockets, he said, "How the hell do you know that he is my son? I remember using protection! For all I know he could be that idiot's son, the one you're working with. What? Did he put you up to this because he doesn't want to be a dad? How the hell can you tell me this when I have seen that little boy nearly every weekend since you returned? Huh?" He pulled his hands out of his pockets and grabbed my shoulders.

I could see he was angry and obviously he had every right to be. Tears stung my eyes and as he shook me alarm bells went off. Pulling my shoulders free I tried to get up, but he pinned me down to the bench.

"Answer me, damn it! What game are you playing at? You know that I want you, so you lay this at my door? If he was my son, surely you would have told me straight away." I received another severe shaking that rattled my teeth and made me wince with pain.

"Let go of me right now!" I shouted, my voice betraying my anger and fear. "He is your son and I didn't know how to tell you. It's not something you can just spring on a person after five years. Plus you broke up with me remember? I always thought that you and Lola were

115

married and had kids. How was I supposed to know that you had broken up with her too?"

"Because I told you the first day we saw each other. I was *honest* which is something you haven't learned in all the years we were friends. I guess I tried to believe you were innocent but the cracks are starting to show. Maybe Ma and Zoe are right. Maybe you did have something to do with the fire all those years ago."

I gasped. "How can you say that? I didn't do it. You were there with me when I received the call. I was standing in front of you when the call came about my dad. How can you forget the day you decided to tell me you were engaged to Lola? I was so excited to tell you the news about the baby. Yes! I knew then. But you had the audacity to tell me that you loved Lola and had already announced the engagement." My voice screeched and tears choked me as I tried to catch my breath.

Anger coursed through my shaking limbs. The stupid flimsy, floral, strappy dress I had decided to wear did nothing to keep me warm as the world seemed to drop in temperature.

"Don't you remember? I begged you to take me to the warehouse to see if my dad was okay and you left me to go on my own. How can you stand there and accuse me when you supposedly knew me so well?"

I tried to shake his iron grip off me. He held on tighter, hurting my biceps with the strength in his calloused hands. I desperately tried to brush away the wetness from my eyes.

"Let me go! You're hurting me you bastard!" I cried, fighting his grip. His face had hardened and his usually soft expression turned brutish with an ugly sneer.

"Or what? You're going to run away again and decide to return with another brat and call it mine? I don't think so. Only if I get something to remember you by, you stuck up bitch! It took me so long to see your pretty little ass. I'm not going to wait that long again."

He pushed me back against the bench, and as much as I kicked and fought, he ended up with his heavy body pressed down on me.

Thunder rumbled above our heads and the first heavy drops of rain fell on my upturned face. The warm wetness soaked my skin as I screamed and punched, landing a fist on his left ear. He roared in pain and slapped me hard, making me see stars. His body couldn't balance on the thin bench without holding on to something more solid than my shoulders, and as I rocked myself to the side, we both toppled over onto the damp sidewalk. The rain splattered down with fury, soaking us to the bone in seconds. The lightning flashes highlighted Jason's angry face as he struggled to hold me to him.

"Hey, what are you doing there?" a voice shouted out from the wet darkness. Splashing footsteps approached us and Jason quickly pushed me aside and leapt to his feet, pulling me up with him. A policeman appeared, looking sternly at both of us, taking in our ruffled, wet clothes.

"Sorry officer, just having some fun with my girlfriend," Jason shouted above the noise of the storm. The wind whipped the line of palm trees behind us into a mad dance that had their limbs bending and swaying to the crescendo of the tropical storm. The policeman glanced at the storm and gestured for us to move on as we couldn't hear anything he said. Jason took the opportunity to snatch my hand and pull me in the direction of his parked car. The slick wetness from the rain helped me pull back and I ran towards the officer who was close to the exit of the park. He jumped in surprise at my touch and looked at the figure of Jason lurking in the shadows, trying to catch up with me.

"Madam are you okay?" he shouted, his dark eyebrows meeting together in a concerned frown.

"No!" I cried. "Please escort me out of this park as I have had a fight with my boyfriend and need to get away."

The policeman took a moment to assess the situation and then gestured for me to follow him out of the park and back onto the main road. Jason was a big guy and a formidable figure when angry or provoked. I had forgotten just how violent he could be when he was upset. The street lights illuminated the wet pavement and the storm raging through the trees and shrubs that were hidden behind the solid hedgerows surrounding Harare Gardens.

The rain was unrelenting and my dress and shoes were soaked. My shivering body shook through fear and not the cold. Once we were closer to the road junction leading up to Karigamombe Centre and to the right down to the Jameson Hotel, the officer asked me what I wanted to do. I thanked him kindly and said I would get a taxi home from the hotel down the road. He bid me a good night after asking if I required his protection any further and briskly walked into the blinding rain back towards the park.

I wondered if he would search for Jason, but didn't hang around to find out. Running down the wet pavement, I sought shelter under the grand entranceway to the

Jameson Hotel. Its sparkling marble steps and bright lights were a welcome sight. Visitors coming in and out didn't hang around, as they too were getting a soaking from the storm. I had to get back to Ma's house before Jason did so that I could take Zachary home.

Realising that all I had in my little purse was some lip gloss and my mobile phone and no money, I groaned in despair. Thinking quickly, I dialled Alex's number, hoping he would be home.

"Hello? Amanda? Where are you?" Alex answered after the second ring.

"Hi! I'm stranded in town and I need your help," I replied. The phone crackled slightly as another flash of lightning lit the dark sky. I hadn't realised I was panting and tried to control my breath.

"Where are you now?" he said, his voice a low growl.

"I'm at the Jameson Hotel. It's just on the corner of Samora Machel and Angwa Street, opposite Karigamombe Centre. Please hurry Alex!" I cried into the phone. If Jason reached Zachary before me, what was the worst he could do? He was angry with me, but I had no idea how he would react to a little child.

CHAPTER ELEVEN

"What the hell are you doing here and where is Zach?" he said. I shivered, my lips chattering as I tried to rub my arms to get warm. My whole body was wetting his car seat. He quickly took off his jacket and draped it around my shoulders, rubbing my outer arms to help me warm up. I winced as he touched the areas where Jason had gripped me.

"Please, we have to go pick him up now. There is no time to explain." With that I gave him directions to Esther's house and he shot off into the night traffic at a terrific speed, as if sensing the predicament I had left Zachary in.

We arrived at the house in record time. Jason's car was nowhere to be seen, just my Toyota, parked where I had left it earlier. Jumping out of the car I ran to the front door, banging on it in my fearful state. Alex was two steps behind me and I tried to ignore his wary stare. The door opened abruptly and Ma peered at us, shock registering on her face when she saw Alex.

"Amanda what are you doing here? Where are Jason, Zach and Zoe?" she asked, still staring at Alex.

"What do you mean? Aren't they here with you?" Alex asked, pushing me to his side and holding me to him as I shivered in the rain. Ma stared with shock at Alex and I quickly introduced them which did nothing to lessen her curious expression. Alex stood fast, holding me close and my shakes seemed to subside with his warmth.

"Mrs Munford, we need to know where Zachary is right this minute!" his authoritative voice boomed above the noise of the thunder.

She ushered us into the lounge where we stood, both dripping on the stained tatty carpet and saw just how shabby the room looked under such severe lighting. A few Christmas trimmings were hanging from the ceiling and added to the claustrophobic feel of the room. I hadn't noticed them before now and could only assume they had started decorating the room tonight. Alex's body stiffened as he took in the surroundings of my grandmother's house. She watched him, her expression sour.

"I don't know who you are mister, but don't come into my house judging me and bossing me around hey!" Her anger filtered into her voice and I quickly stepped forward, touching her arm gently.

"Ma please, we are just worried about Zach. He hasn't spent this much time away from me and Jason didn't ask me if he could take him." What else could I say under the circumstances?

"Well that is his son!" Ma exclaimed. "Okay, so if you're worried, why did you separate from him and let him come home on his own, huh? He said you were with him in the car and you were going to take Zach out as a family for ice cream. Zoe tagged along to join in the fun."

I could hear the intake of Alex's breath but didn't have the courage to glance at his expression. What fun my mind screamed as I tried to stay focused instead of passing out with worry. My body was aching from the battering it had received from Jason and I wanted to find Zachary and run away from this madness.

"Ma, where did they go?" I cried in desperation.

"Oh, just down to the Fife Avenue shops for ice cream at Happy Days!" she said flippantly, turning towards the door as if to throw us out into the dark wet night. "Go get your son and spoil the fun he's having with his father if you must. And you mister, I hope you realise that you are tearing a family apart. We have been separated for so long and now there is a chance of us all being together again. So, just think about that as you flaunt yourself in front of this girl. She never could sit still, this one," Ma continued muttering under her breath.

I felt humiliated as I stormed out of the house and back to the car. It was too much to take in one evening and I desperately wanted my son back, no matter what. Alex opened the car door and walked swiftly out of the rain to get into the driver's side. As I attached my seatbelt, his jacket fell off my shoulders and revealed the bruises on my arms. The car's cabin light highlighted the fingerprint marks left and before I could hide them, Alex gently grabbed my wrist, turning my arm left and right to examine the marks.

"Did he do this to you?" he whispered. I nodded, tears welling up as I tried to control the pain from his examination. He swore under his breath, looking at me and visibly shaking with an anger I had already encountered earlier that evening from another man. I shrugged back against my seat, not too sure what his reaction would be and still reliving Jason's onslaught in the back of my mind.

The light went out automatically in the car, leaving us sitting in the darkness, thunder still rumbling above and the splatter of raindrops hitting the car. His eyes clouded at my reaction to his anger and he gently released my wrist. "I would never hurt you like this Mandy. Trust me!" he said and he started the car, putting his mind to reversing out of the driveway.

I caught sight of Ma watching us from the front door, her face still the picture of a soured woman who had aged bitterly and I felt a great sadness deep within. The truth was seeping out from the pores of my life and everything was shattering around me. I didn't know which way to turn and the confusion and hurt over Jason's anger, Ma's shrewd remarks and Alex's own turmoil left me begging for answers on how to please everyone. The bubbling of my own anger was starting to rise.

We drove at break neck speed to the shopping centre which was only a few miles away and I spotted Jason's car parked in front of the ice cream parlour, highlighted with flashing neon lights that sparkled on the wet tarmac in reds and greens. We got out and made our way to the parlour. The three of them were sitting in a small booth, eating different flavour ice creams. Zach sat happily chatting away to the adults who seemed pre-occupied with each other. Zoe was the first to notice our arrival and sat back in shock, releasing Jason's hand which she had been holding under the table.

Jason's expression was one of pure hatred when he saw Alex standing next to me. His face pulled back into a sneer of a smile as he carelessly threw his arm across the seat behind Zachary's chair, a silent warning against grabbing the child.

"I see you decided to come join the family outing," he said, his muddy brown eyes taking in my rough appearance and Alex's coat covering my damp dress sticking to me. I raised my chin in indifference to his

125

raping stare and ran a shaking hand through my wayward curls, pushing them back out of my face.

"Mummy!" yelled Zachary, as he scrambled from the chair and ran to me. I grabbed him up into a tight hug, holding him close and smelling the dank smell of Ma's house on his clothes and skin. His held me tight and kissed me, eyes welling up with tears. "I missed you so much and Aunty Zo Zo and Jason came to take me out for ice cream. I wanted you to come with us but they said you couldn't come!" he whispered, just loud enough for Alex and I to hear above the noise of the thumping music playing in the parlour.

"Don't worry sweetheart. We are here now. Did you enjoy your ice cream?" I said, holding back the tears of relief that threatened to fall. He nodded and looked at my face, streaks of wetness on his own little cheeks. Zachary turned to Alex and put out his hands as though to go to him and Alex moved closer, receiving a hug around his neck. He put his arms around us both and hugged us close, looking at me above Zachary's curls. His eyes were black granite, hard and unyielding as his jaw muscles worked in an effort to contain his anger.

"Oh what a pretty family picture!" came a sarcastic drawl from the booth. "I guess I was right. My little Bumblebee couldn't keep her sweet ass in one place. So do I still play daddy or will this asshole take my place?" Jason said, hurt and anger flittering through his words.

126

Alex turned to him, stretching his tall body to full height and we could all see his struggle to keep control as his hands flexed open and closed. "No-one can take your place, unless you want them to Jason. You've had your fun tonight. But if you ever pull a stunt like this, or what you did to Amanda earlier, you'll have to answer to me!"

His solid stare dared Jason to make a move, any move that would give him the opportunity to hurt him. Youngster scattered in seats and against the glass windows watched with bated breath as the showdown between two powerful men played out. I stepped back, afraid that Zachary would be hurt in the crossfire and knowing the strength of both men, wanting to be far away if a fight broke out.

Long thin fingers curled round the left bicep of Jason's arm and Zoe wrapped her other hand around his fingers. He glanced down at her, his expression softening as he gazed into her liquid green eyes silently imploring him to stand down. Jason looked up at Alex and as he caught my shocked expression, he wrapped his arms around Zoe's slim body and squeezed her to his side. My disgust seemed to amuse him further because he dragged her back to the booth where they were sitting earlier and snuggled into the corner slipping his hand between her thighs. I couldn't bear anymore and walked out.

Alex followed me out of Happy Days, back to the car. He carefully attached Zach's seatbelt and then insisted on helping me with my own, taking care not to touch the bruises on my arms. The drive home was silent, as quiet as the night. The storm had blown over leaving a freshness to the air and battered wetness to everything. We reached home exhausted and relieved to be on our own turf again. Zachary received his second bath of the evening and was tucked in bed with a soft teddy.

"Mummy? Why does Aunty Zo Zo always stare at me so much?" he asked. His body was curled up next to teddy and I sat on the edge of the bed, gently stroking his damp curls. His face looked pale and drawn.

"I don't know how she stares at your sweetheart. Does it make you feel uncomfortable?" I asked, fear tickling the hairs on the back of my neck.

"No. I just don't like it when she hugs me tight and says that I'm her's!" he mumbled, drifting off to sleep.

What? Zoe can speak? Zachary is hers? What the hell was going on?

CHAPTER TWELVE

Alex heard the muffled sounds of whimpering. The sound rose then drifted into the silent cold night. He sat up in his ruffled bed and rubbed his hand against the stubble on his chin. It was the middle of the night and a chill lingered in the bedroom, giving it an eerie feel. The sound came again, this time a more pronounced cry. Zachary!

Alex leapt out of bed and crossed the passageway to the little boy's bedroom as silently as a shadow. He gently opened the door and watched the sleeping form for a few minutes but no sound came from the bed. The whimpering was coming from the third bedroom…Amanda! He softly closed the door and made his way to the boy's mother's room. Watching her lying in her bed sent his heartbeat soaring. Her hair fanned about her small face which looked so innocent in sleep. Her body barely made an impression in the bed and looked as small as her little boy's.

She twisted in her sleep, groaning and whimpering, her face distorting in pain or fear. Alex's heart skipped a beat and anger beat against his head. That bastard was giving her nightmares. He felt responsible, wanting to gather her into his arms and protect her. He should have known that Jason was Zachary's father. The similarity stared everyone in the face. But that didn't give that asshole the right to abuse her. He should have been there to protect her. She was so fragile, and as much as he tried to hold back, his body drove him closer to the bed.

She twisted again and whimpered in her sleep, pushing invisible villains away from her. Alex needed to touch her, to wake her from the nightmare. He gently shook her, brushing her knotted hair off her face. Tears stuck tendrils to her cheeks and eyes and she moaned. His heart broke at her anguish and without thinking he swept her frail form into his arms. She screamed awake, pushing and fighting him, her face pinched and pale with big frightened eyes, dark with terror.

"It's me Mandy! It's me. Calm down sweetheart. It's okay." His voice deepened as he tried to contain the fury he felt against the man that had caused her harm. Her cold body fit snugly against his bare chest. The thin nightdress could not have kept her warm with such a chill in the air and he wrapped her closer, kissing her forehead, her fluttering eyelids and wet cheeks.

"Please don't cry sweetheart!" he whispered into her hair. More kisses slowly erased the tears from her cheeks, trailing an irresistible path to the tip of her nose, then the corner of her mouth. She lifted her face to him, her eyes a rich pool of flashing emeralds burning with passion. Her cold fingers smoothed down the rigid muscles under his soft golden skin and brought goose bumps along the warm surface.

He breathed in, tensing his abdomen as her hands explored his naked torso. Her inquisitive fingers followed the hairline on his chest. The nightmare disappeared and was replaced with hot, wet desire in the pit of her stomach. Alex's hand stilled on her back and he held his breath, afraid to move forward and fighting common sense that told him to release her. She breathed in his scent, the musky smell of his cologne still lingering on his warm body and could sense his need for permission to continue. She leaned closer to his chest and kissed his golden skin, whispering softly against it.

Alex felt his body heat rise, making it hard to think straight. She felt like an ethereal being, held close to his chest, whispering and kissing his skin so softly. Raging messages were sent to every part of his body and it took all his self-control not to tear the soft material off her deliciously soft skin and ravish her with his mouth. He wanted to be sure, not only of himself but of her. He couldn't bear to see her look at him with the same fear he had seen in the midst of her nightmare only minutes before. She was kissing his neck and had gathered herself up on the bed, still within his arms, kneeling in front of him and kissing her way up to his mouth.

Her breasts were peaked, and he could feel their hard points rubbing against his bare chest as she kissed his open mouth, exploring its depths with her tongue. His hands seemed to find a life of their own, slowly lifting the nightdress so that he could feel her bare skin, stroke her body and enjoy the softness.

"Are you sure you want to do this?" he whispered against her lips.

"Yes," she sighed, setting a fire within him. "Please, don't leave me Alex!" she whispered, barely audibly as she closed her eyes and plunged into a deeper kiss, raising his temperature even higher.

Alex drew her nightdress over her head, exposing her nakedness underneath. He followed her pattern, kissing her along tantalising trails on her body that sent her writhing in passion. He felt her hands removing his pyjama bottoms and assisted her progress. This left them both naked and exposed to each other. Being drunk the last time had made everything hot and passionate but this time, they could feel every emotion, take their time and sense each other's needs.

Alex took his time to follow her golden skin, revelling in its beauty and her shape of body. She rubbed his arms, feeling the strength of his biceps as he sucked and kneaded her breasts, sending her over the edge with want. He trailed his fingers downwards to her core, feeling the inviting wetness and responding with his own body tightening further, begging him to enter her. Separating her legs, he pushed himself into her, feeling her tighten around him, and hearing her moan with pleasure.

Kissing her open mouth, his tongue meshing with hers, he thrust deep into her again and again, feeling the waves of passion envelope them both. She gasped, tightening her grasp on his arms as she reached her climax, sending him past the point of no return as he joined her. Their bodies throbbed together, slowly ebbing and leaving a satiated glow. She hugged herself to him, wrapping her legs tight around him so there was no escape. His arms flexed as he kept most of his weight from crushing her and continued kissing her deeply until they were both breathless.

Gently, they released each other and he rolled onto the side, taking her with him in his arms, wrapping them both in the sheets and blankets that were within reach of the dishevelled bed. Silence permeated the room as they lay together, drifting slowly into a peaceful sleep.

Alex didn't want to think of tomorrow or the day after that. He didn't want to face the questions he needed to ask her about her family and her past. It was enough to have her safe in his arms, away from the dangers of the world. The thought of Amanda and Zachary leaving once the trip was over made him shiver and he hugged her tightly to him. This woman seemed to fill a void in his life that he had refused to acknowledge, let alone challenge.

Hell, Sienna's memory seemed to exist on a different plane and the guilt he had eating away at his gut still gnawed with a vengeance, but the warmth in his chest filtered it to a tolerable level. He felt a need to keep her to him, watch her laugh and smile and fill him with a happiness he had never felt before. Even with Sienna! That thought shocked him awake. He felt a deeper affection for Amanda and her son that touched regions he had been unaware even existed in his heart. He never imagined that to be possible. Did she feel the same way? Was it worth the risk of finding out, only to have his heart smashed to pieces again?

The next morning brought aches and pains in my arms and back. The bruises were more visible in the light of day. Questions I had floating around in my head had me tossing and turning the night before, and I needed answers. If Zoe could talk, why was she pretending that she couldn't communicate with people? Did Ma and Jason know? Were they all in on her little secret and why? I had to go back to find out the answers and to retrieve my car.

Alex had returned to his room in the early hours of the morning. He seemed to avoid me at breakfast and disappeared straight after. His car was gone by the time I was out of the shower, so I assumed he had made an early start to the day to avoid discussing the awkward conversation of what exactly was happening between us.

The rain had stopped and the air smelled crisp and clean. All the leaves seemed to glow with a fresh washed look, and the sound of the birds chirruping to each other was a beautiful melody. The stones were sparkling with residual drops of water, as we stomped through little pocket puddles towards the awaiting taxi that would take Zach and I back to Ma's house.

My head was buzzing with confusion on how to tackle a family that seemed so loving one minute and complete strangers the next. Could five years change people so drastically? Or maybe the lies had always been there and I was blind to them; so wrapped up in my own little

135

world, and being the selfish person I was, I wouldn't have noticed subtle things in my family. The gate was locked and it took Kumbi a while to answer the insistent hooting of the taxi driver. The rest of the street seemed deserted. At last the gate reluctantly opened and we walked in, waving thanks to the retreating taxi driver.

Kumbi was silent, and had a sullen expression when I asked her where the family was. She was usually so friendly and sweet; I wondered what they could have said to make her react this way. Zoe and Ma were in the kitchen, preparing an early lunch, and they seemed surprised at my early return. Zoe's surly expression and curled sneering lips made the hairs stand up on the back of my neck. I regretted the decision of coming here without Alex. What if Jason came back and I had no protection from these women? They felt like strangers to me. The tension in the hot kitchen made me move closer to the door, keeping Zach tight against my side. The warm family feeling was gone. Again.

"Mandy ma, it's so nice to see you safe and sound. I'm sorry about yesterday. I honestly thought you were with Jason when he came to pick up Zachary." Ma nervously twisted her hands, edging closer to me. "Are you cross with me Ma?" she asked, scratching the bald spot just behind her ear.

"No Ma, I'm not cross anymore," I replied, trying to keep my expression neutral. My eyes kept darting to

Zoe who seemed amused at my discomfort. It made me angry and I straightened my back, ready to fight anything. "Ma, did you know that Zoe can talk?" She gasped, anger flashing in her hazel green eyes.

"What? Don't be silly Mandy. You know that Zoe hasn't spoken since the fire," said Ma in exasperation. "What would make you ask something like that?" She glanced back at Zoe who gave her an innocent hurt look. Anger swelled in my chest and filled my lungs with hot air. Visions of Jason's hand wrapped around her inner thigh, stroking her darkness burned with ferocity.

"Oh I don't know. Maybe because I heard her speak!" I said. Both women looked at me queerly.

"When did you hear her speak, Amanda?" I could hear Ma's tone change and could see she was upset too. Her hunched back straightened slightly and the scratching stopped. Zoe looked ready to claw my eyes out. Sharp white teeth poked out from thin pink lips which pulled down on the one side of her face.

"I heard her speaking to Zach the other day when we came over for lunch," I lied, not wanting Zoe to know that Zach had told me.

"That's impossible Amanda. If that is all you came here to ask, then you had better go. You caused enough trouble last night with that other boy. What kind of girl goes on a date with one boy and comes back with another? Haven't I taught you to respect yourself? I'm really cross with your behaviour. And to think that your son watches you acting like a tramp!"

I stuttered, too upset to reply and incensed to have my little sister smirk in the background, knowing full well her part played in the whole event.

"So I guess you think it is okay for Jason and Zoe to be a couple then?"

Gasp!

"Amanda! Have you gone mad? What's wrong with you today? Jason is like a big brother to Zoe. He has cared for her since she left the hospital, dying from her wounds. He's the only one that helped save your father's business and without him we would never have survived this long in this house. You run away after destroying your family and think you can come back with your bastard child, accusing your poor innocent sister of things I could only see you doing! Get out! And don't come back until you're ready to apologise to Jason and Zoe."

I had never seen my grandmother angry and her words cut through me. Zach whimpered next to me and snapped me out of my shock. Without wasting another minute in an unwelcome house, I stormed out, quickly unlocking the car and loading Zachary into the back seat.

The sun beat down on my back, whilst a chill lingered deep in my bones. What a mistake to come back to this god-forsaken country and to try to make amends for my past. No-one believed me. I did not start that damn fire, but I was going to find out who did. The best place would be the police. They had to have a record of the night and if I could piece together the time the fire started and prove that I had no part in the devastation, it was one step closer to clearing my past. I risked them opening up a case against me, but it would be worth the risk if my name was cleared. Maybe I could trust Alex enough to ask him to help me. Maybe? I slept with the man and trusted him with my son. I should give him more credit than that.

The roads were still quiet as we zoomed back to Avondale, determined to get a head start on my investigation. There was not much time left before we returned to England, and I wanted to clear my name before it was too late. Jason could go to hell if he thought he was going to get his hands on Zachary. I would rather die than let him have my son.

As for Zoe, I would find out what her game was and expose her for the fraudulent little witch that she was, especially her relationship with Jason. Ma would see that I am not a little tramp and traitor. None of my friends wanted to know me. None of my friends had made the effort to get back into contact, and I knew why. They all thought the same thing as my family. I was an accused leper that no-one wanted to touch.

 The roads were filled with purple Jacaranda flowers, and as the wheels drove over them, they gave out a loud POPPING sound! The sight of the purple flowers draping down over the avenue and the velvet carpet of fallen flowers on the road had a soothing effect on me. I had forgotten how beautiful the rainy season could be in November. Jacaranda season! As I approached the cross road separating Milton Park from Avondale, the slickness of the flowers made the wheels skid slightly. I tried to pump the brakes, but nothing happened. Our car was still moving forward at a faster pace than anticipated, and I could see a truck approaching the junction from the right at great speed.

Thinking fast I pulled up the handbrake, but nothing happened! The truck skidded across the open junction, jack knifing in an attempt to avoid hitting us. Our car broached the centre at the same time, brakes squealing, and the heart-wrenching sound of tyres burning on the tarmac in a frenzy to stop. A loud crash announced impact, and I watched the load from the truck lurch towards us in a graceful arch.

Crunching metal mixed with the smell of gasoline and terrified screams coming from the back of the car. Zach! The world turned into a frenzy. The truck hit the side of the car sending it into a mad spin across the road where a light post stopped our crazy dance with a smash. Everything slowed, as I looked around to see Zach flicking forward, his small arms reaching out to me and his mouth a perfect 'O' shape matching his wide terrified eyes, then catapulting back with the snap of the seatbelt before darkness enveloped the world. The smell of burning stayed with me in the darkness, as did the muffled sound of people screaming and the distant sirens approaching.

CHAPTER THIRTEEN

BEEP! BEEP! BEEP!

My eyes felt so heavy, and whenever I tried to open them, they blurred over so it was hard to make out anything around me. Just that sound...

BEEP! BEEP! BEEP!

And, the smell of antiseptic was everywhere. Where was I? I could feel my body hurting so badly with even the slightest movement, but the overpowering urge to sleep helped me slip back into a world of numbness and silence. Soft voices permeated the silence every now and then, as shadows seemed to stalk my peripheral view. Everything seemed so confused and sleepy. I have to get back to sleep.

"I saw her eyes move! I'm sure she's awake Ma!"

"Yes! Yes! I see it! Her eyes moved and tried to open. Manda Ma, can you hear us? Please open your eyes my girl!"

Sniff. Sniff.

"Well, her shoulder is badly damaged. She is lucky that the bruising on her legs will be gone in a couple of weeks."

"What about her eyes?   Why won't she open them properly doctor?"

"It might have been the impact to her head. We will have to examine her sight once she recovers consciousness fully. However, all in all she is a very lucky young lady. A pity about her son though."

BEEP! BEEP! BEEP!

My eyes are clearing and I can make out shapes walking around a white room. The clarity is still rubbish but the sounds are much more consistent. I can hear Ma's voice, fussing and crying, and I can feel her holding my hand. Such warm hands. Deep voices consoling her and my body being shifted, as needles are stuck in and my body is washed. Sleep is still calling me back to a wonderful abyss where everything stops and the confusion ends.

ZACHARY!!

Oh my God! My son! He was in the car, and I could hear him screaming in the back as the truck hit us. My eyes. I have to open my eyes. They burn, as I try to focus on my surroundings. My throat is dry, and it feels as though something is stuck in it. I gag, trying to swallow. I can hear the machines going frantic next to my bed. Darkness again.

"Amanda, can you hear me? If you can, please open your eyes."

A piercing light is shone into them and I blink away the tears and try to focus. The doctor prods and pokes for as long as I can remember and my throat is constricting before I have a chance to ask my question.

"Wh...where is my son?" my voice rasps out, sounding foreign to my ears.

"He wasn't hurt bad and is resting in the Children's Ward where we can monitor him. Do you remember what happened?"

I can just focus on the doctor's face and the grim lines around his mouth and eyes.

"I was driving and my car ... crashed. Broken glass and a big truck hit us," I said, gasping at the dryness in my throat. My throat felt as though I had been screaming for days on end.

"Yes, that is right. The truck that hit you sent your car spinning into a lamp post. Unfortunately the driver ran away from the scene and has not yet been found. The police will be in later today to take a statement from you if you feel strong enough."

More prodding and poking. My gown is straightened and I feel the coolness of my pillow again.

"Visitors are only allowed for a short while until I'm sure you can handle it, okay?" the doctor says in his no-nonsense way. "They are already here and I'll send them in one at a time, but don't let them tire you out, okay?"

"Yes. Thank you," I manage and close my eyes for a moment. Everything is so bright and I feel broken.

"Hi Mandy love. How are you feeling?"

I open my eyes and there is Jason. Tall, strong with his muscles flexing under his tight t-shirt, he comes forward and holds my hand with a gentleness I appreciate.

145

"Hey! Thanks for coming to see me." I rasp out an automatic response, trying to swallow.

"Don't talk too much. The doctors have had you fitted with a pipe for the past week and they said it would be painful for you to talk at first. I'm so sorry this happened to you my love. We've got so much to talk about once you're better."

He glances behind him with a slight frown on his face. I can't see who he is looking at but he turns back to me and smiles, his brown eyes dancing with light.

"You've been a naughty girl. Ma told me about your visit before the accident. Why didn't you tell me? I would have been there and maybe this would never have happened."

My confusion makes my blink as the searing light burns through my skull. What visit? To where?

Another glance behind him and a nod.

"Okay, I have to go now, but I'll come see you again tomorrow. I love you bumble bee!" He reaches forward and kisses me. It's like I'm 17 again and we're a couple. I feel his warmth and it makes a bubble of happiness erupt under all the pain. I smile at him. He disappears and I close my eyes.

Warm hands envelope mine and I open my groggy eyes to stare at hard granite and a grim face with haggard lines. Alex stares down at me, as though I have stolen his favourite pony, but all I can do is to stare back at him. My heart beats faster, and I feel uncomfortable lying there with his eyes searching mine for answers to questions I don't know.

"I was worried about you," he manages through tight lips. His skin looks sallow as though he hasn't been kissed by the sun for a while and his black curly hair has a crazy look about it as though he has been sleeping rough.

"I'm sorry," I whisper, thinking he is angry that I crashed the rental car. We must be over a month in the country and there is so much more work to do. Or was it two weeks? I can't remember and trying to remember is hurting my head. I have to break through this horrible hazy feeling and think clearly.

Wait. A few weeks? Jason attacking me and seducing Zoe. Angry words with Ma and Zoe's sneakiness. I remember jumbled patterns of questions I wanted answered and the need to tell Alex.

147

"I was driving ..." I try to clear my throat but the raspy sound continues. "I tried to stop, but ... the truck came..."

I close my eyes as the image of the truck skidding towards us suddenly emerges like a rush of cold water against my skin. I feel tears welling up and I want to look away but I can feel Alex gently brushing away the tears.

"Please don't cry. It wasn't your fault. I didn't mean to make you cry Amanda." His gruff voice breaks slightly and I look up to see his face so drawn and tired.

I try to reach out to stroke his cheek, and he reaches forward to my shaking hand. I stroke his bent head and can feel his hair is greasy and definitely not brushed. His chin is covered with a ragged beard, and he doesn't look anything like the Alex I know.

"Please check on Zachary," I whisper, as he lifts his head to look at me.

"I will. I have taken care of him, so don't worry. Your grandmother has been standing vigil over him as well as your sister and ... Zachary's father," he replies, a grim expression returning to his face. "Why didn't you tell me your secrets Amanda?"

I close my eyes, trying to block out his anger. I feel the warmth leave my fingers.

"Mandy, my girl! Are you awake?" Esther's voice permeates through my sleepiness.

"Hi Ma! Yes, yes I am awake," I say feeling like a small child again.

"Oh my girl, you gave me such a fright. How could you do that? We were so worried about you two. My God, the poor child. He is so small to go through so much. But don't worry, you will both be okay now!" she continues, crying and sniffing.

"Ma, I'm so tired," I reply. I am trying to keep my eyes open but their resistance to light is fading and I can feel myself falling away into the abyss again.

Silence and complete peace. For how long?

Zoe watched her helpless nephew take in painful breaths and exhale them with the same torment as the machines monitored his progress. She watched as the doctors and nurses resuscitated him, while her anger burnt deep and furious. This was Amanda's fault. She never cared for anyone in her life and was so negligent; she didn't see when she hurt people. This little child was suffering the same way she had suffered years ago, fighting for her life with severe burns to her face and body. Did Amanda even care? No! She didn't even bother stopping in her big escape to think about the sister she left behind to pay for her indiscretions.

Yes, Zoe knew that Amanda had been in the warehouse that fateful night and had followed her. No-one noticed Zoe. She was as invisible now, as she had been then. No-one saw her following Jason and Lola, watching Jason play both girls like a fiddle. Only she knew that Jason couldn't find what he was looking for in both those girls.

He was her best friend, the guy she could hang out with anytime without judgement. All those nights spent at his house listening to him go on about life and expectations, sharing dreams together. Surely he knew how much their friendship meant to her. Of course he did. Why else would he have taken her under his wing after the fire? Why else would he have stepped up to help her parents when they were threatened with the loss of their business, and when they couldn't bear to be near Zoe, even though she craved their comfort and understanding?

He needed guidance, the same way he did years ago when he started messing around with her sister and Lola. He was a self-centred, arrogant pig that had taken his special friendship with her and used it to get into Amanda's pants! Zoe closed her eyes as she pictured his passion with both girls, whispering promises of a future together with each girl as they lay in his arms, hidden from responsibility in his secret hideout only she, Zoe, had the right to be in. Resentment rose within her. No-one saw her watching. No-one cared. Only Jason.

He loved her and was only using them. He needed her more than he needed them. She taught him a lesson then and it was time to remind him how important she still remained, even if the witch had returned with their son. She had created that link and she could destroy it just as easily. Maybe it was time to get rid of her ridiculous sister for good.

A silvery smile crept across her beautifully ugly face, hazel eyes glittering with anticipation. Zoe knew what to do. No-one ever saw her coming.

CHAPTER FOURTEEN

Two weeks had passed and Amanda was looking forward to being released from this hell soon. She had been cooped up in the hospital all that time, recovering from bruising to the legs, a broken arm, and a slight concussion. The visitors that came through the door were faces she had not seen for years; childhood friends now sporting facial hair, or carrying children with full bodies showing the age difference of when she knew them compared to now. The accident had closed the chasm separating them from her, and she gladly accepted their titbits of friendship which shortened the hours of the day until it was time for Alex and Zach to come visit.

The rainy season had settled in and torrential storms blew outside the hospital window. The humid heat of the day had cooled drastically, giving everything a fresh smell, as twinkling drops glittered from every leaf that swayed in the wind's waltz of a never ending dance. Visitors carried their wet umbrellas through the hospital corridors, leaving snail trails of droplets which the janitors followed with resigned diligence. Nurses bustled around speaking Shona and laughing happily in the recovery wing, making visitors and patients feel uplifted by the sounds of assured joy.

Alex was by her side as often as he could manage whilst finishing off the last property transfers and court appearances for the Partels' business. The pressure was on to ensure the transfers would be complete, or at least in an expedited process before the Christmas pace took over the town. Things slowed to a painful speed once December rolled in and most families took off to holidays around the world, or visited their in-laws around the country. Mr Ismail was happy with the progress made, and Alex made sure to report back to Jennifer in the UK to keep her in the loop too. Amanda used their time together to slowly explain the turn of events that had led her to running away from her past life and her involvement with Jason.

It was too painful to dwell over it for too long, and Alex's expression showed just how uncomfortable he was with discussing her previous lover. She felt the need to tell him her doubts about Zoe and the fact that she was hiding her ability to speak. They both knew that Zoe had a malicious streak, but just how far would she go to hurt Amanda and why? Alex promised her that he would look out for Zachary and visit him as often as possible when he wasn't with her.

His closeness to her and the warmth emanating from his strong sturdy presence reassured Amanda that maybe things would be alright after all. After the initial scare which held Zachary in hospital for a week, his fast recovery from a bruised arm and slight breathing problems from the seatbelt pulling across his ribs meant he could leave the hospital with Alex soon. She felt a huge weight of relief knowing that he would take care of her son as though Zachary was his own.

Jason was a constant visitor too, with apologies over his rogue behaviour and flagrant flirtation with Zoe. She kept quiet through the apologies, reliving the awful night when she told him Zach was his son. She groaned inwardly, as the only other man she had ever had sex with compared her to her sister and how sweet and innocent Zoe appeared to be in everyone's eyes.

He begged her to forgive his insecurities, and he admitted that using her own sister to make her jealous was an act of cowardice. He assumed from her silent withdrawal that all was forgiven. Zachary was his son, and he wanted to do right by him. That did not necessarily mean he wanted to take an active part in his son's life and excused himself on that front by claiming work and the responsibility of looking after Amanda's family was enough to keep him busy. Amanda was silently relieved that Jason didn't want to be an active father.

The thought of Jason having any influence over her son made her stomach turn. What had she seen in such a shallow man? Granted, she had been young, and they were friends, but she had never felt a burning passion or love for him and had only consented to sleep with him because he had persisted for so long, and she was a bit curious about it. It was one of her deepest regrets with a happy consequence.   Her experience with Jason had never been one to remember, even though it had left her with Zachary, the gem of her life.

She recalled how rough his hands were when they touched her skin, and how he seemed to want to subdue her on the bed they shared for those few hours of passion. It was over before she knew it, while the pain after felt just as extreme as the shame. She remembered her utter humiliation when he announced that he had been going out with Lola all that time and that Lola was pregnant which meant only one thing. He had enjoyed two girls at the same time, abusing friendships in both relationships and subjecting them to the shame of falling pregnant, even though he had used protection.

No. Jason was a person she would be happy to evict out of her life, and she intended on telling him this on his next visit to the hospital. She loved Alex. Her heart sang when he was close. The strength from his broad shoulders that held her and kept her warm and safe made her feel like she was the only woman in the world. The two glorious times she had been lucky enough to make love to him had made her world turn upside down. Her inexperience in bed had not prepared her for his passion, overwhelming her being and sending her to heights of passion never reached before. His compassion and patience with everyone he dealt with, and his open heart that he gave freely to Zachary made her want to run to him and hold on tight, never letting go.

Nevertheless, she knew in her heart that he didn't trust her. He still had too many questions about her past that she didn't have the answers to, and it frustrated her to think that the doubt that shone out of his eyes whenever he asked her questions made her feel like a fraud. Amanda wanted Alex to look at her with an open heart also, and to love her for who she was and not her past. That would never happen unless she uncovered the answers to the questions he constantly raised about her past. Jason could answer those questions if he chose to since he had been with the family all this time. It was time to set the record straight.

Esther, on the other hand, seemed determined to let father and son know each other and started a secret war to take Zachary away from Alex. Without notice to Alex or Amanda, Esther had made sure that Zachary was released from hospital into her care using her grandmother status and the fact that Alex was no blood relation to the child. The doctors saw nothing wrong with this and happily gave him over for full rest and recuperation at home with Grandma! No amount of phone calls from Amanda in the hospital could make her change her mind and the threat of involving the police only served to make her play her hand. She cried on the phone, accusing Amanda of not loving her family and allowing them to help her – again. The hurt she managed to push through the receiver left Amanda reeling with indecision.

Alex ground his teeth in vexation but knew that the grandmother had a grip on her granddaughter he couldn't fight. After making a call to David Gallia at the police station, his friend advised him to step away from the situation. No authority liked to interfere in a family where they were trying to mend bridges. Besides, Alex Edwards had no rights to the child, as he was not the blood father. No, David was adamant that no good would come from interfering in family affairs.

He had more news for his friend about the accident but chose not to share more over the phone, as Alex seemed pre-occupied with the idea that the grandmother would hurt Amanda's son. He ended the conversation with a niggling feeling that Alex knew more than he cared to share. David decided it was time to start digging further into Esther Munford's past, as he had only investigated the direct family. It was time to see what skeletons the old woman held in her closet that could scare his friend so much.

Alex was angry. He ended his conversation with his short, bald friend and felt as though nothing had been achieved. No-one seemed to see the torture that Zach would go through at the house. Only he and Amanda knew, and they didn't dare cause friction in case Zoe retaliated and hurt Zach whilst in the house. He knew he should have mentioned something to David, but he couldn't bring himself to share Amanda's secrets; not without her permission first.

They had to find out more about Zoe, but putting the police onto her might raise enquiries that alerted Zoe to their quiet investigation. He couldn't risk it. He had played into the hands of David though, giving more emotion on his distrust of Esther Munford than he had wanted to. There was nothing he could do about it now. It was more important to try and get Zachary back safe and sound.

Hospital visits from Esther, Zoe, and Zach came fewer and further between, as Amanda's strained face and decelerating recovery worried the doctors as much as Alex. For the second time in his life, the devastating realisation that Alex was on the cusp of losing the ones he loved again drove him over the edge. Waiting be damned! He would get Zach whichever way was necessary and if David or the police couldn't help him, he would go himself.

After sitting outside the house from eight in the morning, hooting and banging at the gate till the neighbours started coming out of their yards to stare at the crazy man making noise down a quiet suburban street, the gate finally opened. He drove through it, barely acknowledging Kumbi's sad face and the hatred in Zoe's eyes as she stood waiting at the end of the driveway.

"What do you want Mr Edwards?" she asked through gritted teeth. Her voice was smooth and soft. Her eyes sparkled in the morning sun, setting off her cat-like features under straightened glossy brown hair.

"I came here to make sure that Zach is okay," he replied, trying to keep his shock at hearing her speak to himself. Amanda had discussed it at great length, but actually hearing her voice sent chills down his spine.

Zach ran out into the dappled sunshine and shrieked with happiness when he saw Alex standing by the car. He ran at full speed into Alex's waiting arms and was tossed high in the air, and then caught in a massive bear hug. Tears flowed as they gripped each other tight and asked if either one was okay. Zach smelt slightly stale and his usually soft brown curls looked knotted and unkempt. He stroked Alex's face with little fingers and his sad wet eyes spoke of unsaid tales that brought raging anger to the front of Alex's head in a red flush.

"What have you done to this child?" he growled at Zoe who had been watching with intense interest at the display of affection between man and child.

She gave a slow crooked smile and cocked one hand on her hip showing just how thin and sinewy she looked. Her eyes shot out flecks of green anger.

"You mean my child? Oh, the little brat doesn't like to listen, so he needs to learn proper manners. That's all!" she sniggered, looking at Zachary's frightened face.

Footsteps sounded on the pathway leading from the side of the house, and Zoe transformed her ugly expression into a sanguine angelic repose, straightening her posture to one of prim innocence. Esther appeared and glared at Alex as though he was Satan himself. He couldn't contain his frustration at Zoe's award-winning performance of innocence. Amanda was right. Her sister, though just as beautiful, was bewitchingly evil.

"What do you think you are doing here?" Esther Munford half shrieked, reaching forward while prying Zachary from Alex's reluctant arms. Zachary cried and scratched to crawl his way back into the safety of the big man's arms.

"Let the poor child go!" Esther yelled, mistaking Zach's struggle and Alex's hold on him to prevent him falling between them, as the reason for Zach's reluctance to go to her.

"He doesn't want to go to you crazy woman!" an irritated Alex shouted in frustrated fury. What had they done to the child to make him this afraid?

With a final tug, she pried him from Alex's arms, and Zoe snatched him up before he could protest further. She leaped out of reach and ran back to the house with the howling child. Alex felt his heart wrench out as he thought of the little boy whose face told him that all was not well in his world. The hatred for these crazy people that Amanda called family was immeasurable, and he wanted to run into that house, snatch Zachary up and run. But he knew if he did that, the police would be on his tail and he would end up as someone's bitch in the notorious Chikurubi Prison faster than you could say AIDS! He stared at the grey haired harpy in front of him and wondered how, for the hundredth time since first meeting her, Amanda could be related to such a person.

"Don't even think of taking him away from us, you home wrecker!" growled Esther. "I don't know why you insist on coming here every day, making noise outside our gate and worrying the neighbours. There is nothing for you here that belongs to you. Get that in your thick head and get the hell off my property!" she shrieked.

"I will keep on coming here until Amanda is out of that damn hospital and able to take back her child to safety. I don't know what you or that witch Zoe is doing and saying to him, but I won't let it keep happening. He is only a child. You should be taking better care of him."

"What the hell do you mean what *we* say to him? Zoe can't say anything to him! She loves him to distraction and probably takes better care of him than his own mother did!" Esther shook her hands at him in uncontrolled anger, her thin frail body looking as though it would crumble under the strain. "Now get out!"

Alex thought better than to argue further with this irate woman. He didn't know the layout of the house, and they could have Zach held in any of the rooms. He was with Zoe, the worst of his fears. Retreat was the only way forward. At least he had seen Zach and knew that even though things were bad, the little guy had seen him and knew he was there working...no, fighting to get him back.

There was still some work outstanding on the Partel case and time was running out. He had to leave this woman and her dangerous granddaughter before he did something drastic. David would have more answers for him on this family, and he could move forward with better information on what his enemy had under their crazy hoods. Getting out of the house was easier and this time he noted Kumbi's sad farewell as he drove away from what he described as *'the mad house'* to himself.

"The files pertaining to the Glenson Factory fire were definitely tampered with," said Alex's ex-police officer friend. "I managed to locate a police report that seemed a bit strange at the time, but with the right palm grease, was opened from the archives. It contained details pertaining to a car accident in the Borrowdale area involving a car and a jogger. It was a simple hit and run case, but the injuries sustained by the jogger grabbed my attention."

Alex inhaled sharply at the other end of the line and David stopped.

"Are you alright Alex?" he asked, knowing that the news he was about to give his friend would answer questions that Alex had searched for over the past few years. He rubbed his bald head and sighed to himself. This job was never easy, especially when it involved friends.

"Yeah! Yeah! Keep going David," was Alex's hollow reply.

"The witness at the incident reported a woman in her early twenties was jogging when a car jumped the traffic light on the Borrowdale Road and hit her at full impact. The body was thrown a couple of metres, and she was declared dead at the scene. What was strange was the fact that the coroner's initial report had an addendum of injuries that included severe burns to the victims' arms and face. The victim had died from smoke inhalation. That could have only occurred if the victim had been in a burning building and not a road accident."

"So what you're saying is that this victim could have been at the site of the fire and someone tried to cover up her existence?" asked Alex, his voice betraying his hurt and anger.

"Yes!" came the short response. "I think that your wife may have been the victim that we are talking about and she may have been a witness to the Glenson Fire."

Alex sat back in his chair and exhaled a deep breath. After five years of hitting his head against bureaucratic dead ends he was one step closer to the truth. Unfortunately, that truth was making Amanda look more and more likely to be his wife's killer! The same woman that had managed to pull him out of a dark, solitary cold world and back into the warmth. He closed his eyes, pinching the bridge of his nose. How could you love someone that might have murdered the woman you claimed to love forever?

"Alex, are you still there?"

"Yes, sorry David. I just needed a moment to take all this in. So, what we know is that Amanda Glenson started a fire at the family business on the night of May 16th, trapping her sister in the inferno and killing the only witness to her crime, who also happens to be my late wife, Sienna?"

"Unfortunately, the evidence is piling up that way. The only thing I can't understand is how the little sister got out of the fire with such severe burns. Could be that maybe your wife tried to help her out but sustained such severe injuries, she couldn't make it out herself," pondered David.

"There is that possibility. I'm going to have to ask Zoe myself and find out the truth, Dave. Look, thanks for all your help in this investigation. I owe you one mate." Alex ended the conversation with a heavy heart. What would Sienna be doing on the other side of town? She had an old apartment close to the old burnt warehouse but that had been rented out at the time of the accident. Unless it wasn't and she had gone there to spend the night.

Alex's memory took him back to that morning together before he left for Los Angeles many years ago. She was so warm and beautiful, her long black hair tickling his chest and arms, as she lay on top of him telling him how much she loved him. He remembered thinking he was going to miss his flight if he didn't get up, but was so reluctant to remove this beautiful creature that he was lucky enough to share the rest of his life with from his warm embrace. They made love again, sweet magical love that told him in no uncertain terms how much this woman loved him. She giggled as he left the bed in a rush, running into the shower and dressing at hyper speed to be ready for the taxi taking him to the airport.

Then it hit him. Sienna had mentioned her own trip to the apartment whilst he was away to sort through things she had left in storage since the tenants had moved out unexpectedly. She had joked about living alone again without him and he had turned to snatch her warm sexy body from the bed, kissing her passionately and threatening to come find her wherever she was so she could never escape him. They had laughed and he had rushed off, not taking her seriously. That had been the last time he had seen his loving wife.

CHAPTER FIFTEEN

Alex dialled the number for the Honey Drive house and asked to speak with Esther. She was not in. Kumbi informed him that Zoe was at home, as Zachary was not feeling well and did not go to school. Alex told her to be ready at the gate as he was coming over right away. She mumbled an incoherent answer in her own language and cut the call short.

Time felt like it was running out. The pieces of the puzzle were falling into place. What if it was true that Amanda had killed his wife? He had promised to protect her and she trusted him. She was in such a vulnerable position now with her crazy family and needed someone close to protect her. Could he trust her? He prayed that Zoe held the answers he desperately needed to solve this mystery and hopefully free his wife's memory forever.

Driving over to their house only took 10 minutes and he hooted at the gate until Kumbi popped her head round and quickly opened it to let him drive the car in and park on the gravel close to the front veranda. The air felt light and fresh on his heated skin, giving him a moment to cool his heels before entering the semi-darkness of the interior of the house. It felt like the first time he had stepped over the threshold, claustrophobic with all the old carpets layering the floor and the overstuffed sofas trying desperately to hold their contents in check whilst some bits escaped. He waited close to the front door, calling out for Zoe and hoping she could hear him. Little footsteps tip tapped from somewhere in the house, and as they came closer he knew it was Zachary's light footsteps.

"Alex!" Zach squealed with delight and ran straight into his waiting arms. Alex held him close and could smell the surroundings clinging to his little body, stale and sweaty. He could feel the little boy's bones as he observed the small drawn face had dark circles under each eye. Amanda's heart would break if she knew her son was living like this, but there was nothing he could do about it whilst she was still in hospital. Her release was coming soon enough, but with all the questions Alex had to answer surrounding her and her family, he was a bit relieved that she had to stay put and couldn't run away again.

"I missed you and Mummy so much," said the soft voice, tears sparkling in big brown eyes. "You said you would look after Mummy!" Zachary's big brown eyes looked questioningly into Alex's dark eyes. "Is she better now?"

Alex tried to swallow the lump growing in his throat. Before he had a chance to answer, a sound of someone's entry to the lounge made him turn. Zoe had appeared, wearing a short mini skirt and a half top that left nothing to the imagination. What the hell was she doing dressed like that around a little child? He was tempted to forget about the burning questions he had and take flight with Zachary. Zoe crawled under his skin every time she came into close proximity and he could feel himself taking a step back towards the front door as she sauntered closer to him.

"Hi Zoe. Sorry if I caught you at a bad time," Alex said gruffly, making a point of looking at the good side of her face and nowhere past her neckline. She giggled, acknowledging his discomfort at her choice of clothing and smiled a wicked, sensuous smile that made her hazel green eyes glitter with vicious amusement.

"Zachary, go find Kumbi and tell her to put you on the bike" came the sharp response, her voice as clear to hear as a loud bell.

Her smooth voice turned deep and crackled a bit, but completely audible. Zachary wiggled down Alex's body and made his way past Zoe to the kitchen. His voice could be heard outside talking to Kumbi. Alex ran a shaky hand through his dark hair. What else was Zoe hiding?

"Shall we sit down Alex? I'm sure you have some burning questions you'd like me to answer," she said, coming forward and linking her arm through his. She led him to the overstuffed sofa furthest away from the small television in the corner and pulled him down next to her. The chair squeaked in protest and Zoe's skirt fluttered up slightly, closer to the tops of her legs. She did nothing to pull it down, and she turned slightly towards Alex as he tried to put a little distance between them, but he was trapped by the armrest of the sofa. He could feel her hand on his thigh, travelling upwards towards his crotch. He dared not look down, as her top had fallen forward and revealed the swell of her youthful breasts, and the peaks of her bare nipples under the thin t-shirt showed clearly.

"So, Mr Alex Edwards, who is so in love with my sister, what do you want from little ol' me?" she sighed into his ear, leaning closer still.

Alex grabbed her hand before she could continue her upward stroke of his leg. He looked at her eyes and could see the madness hidden behind the layers of contempt and attempted seduction.

"What the hell are you playing at Zoe? I came here to ask you about the fire. I want to know what happened. And why the hell did you lie to your family saying that you couldn't speak?" he replied through clenched teeth. His anger was hitting him in waves, and he had to control it or this crazy woman could snap and do anything. She might even hurt Zach.

"Well where should I start? Shall I tell you about your darling Amanda and how she always had to get every boy's attention? Shall I tell you what a slut she was, flirting with anything that had a dick just to dump them and move on? Is that what you want to hear or would you prefer to hear about how she left me in a warehouse to burn, so that the whore could be with my boyfriend?" was the hoarse answer.

He gulped at her pure hatred and straightened up, still trying to distance himself from her claws, his big frame giving no leeway to aid his escape from her close proximity.

"I tell you what. Let me start with how Amanda and I grew up. She was the beautiful one that everyone loved, and I was always second best. She was good at school, sports, anything she bloody well touched! I used to admire her so much and yes, I even loved her. But, as we grew older, I got tired of watching her flaunt herself with all the boys. She never took the time to find out whom I liked, what I loved."

Alex watched as Zoe seemed to stare into the distant past, anger and hatred contorting the beautiful side of her face.

"She took him from me, even though she never loved him. He was so intense, so clever and loving. And she just used him, like all the others."

"Who, Zoe? Who did she take?" Alex asked.

Zoe frowned, focusing her eyes back on Alex. She gave a secretive smile and leaned against his chest, brushing her breasts against him and whispered, "She thinks I can't have you, but I can. I can take what she loves away just as easily as she did it to me." Her free hand slowly dove its way to Alex's crotch and he gasped as she grabbed him through his chinos and squeezed. His body tried not to react, but her wicked eyes gleamed with seduction, and her bare breasts stroked him across his chest, sending an erotic signal straight down.

He pushed her off and stood up shaking.

"What the fuck do you think this is? A game? I want to know what the hell happened the night of the fire Zoe and you're going to tell me now!" he said, stepping towards her sprawled body where he had thrown her off.

She laughed a guttural laugh and stretched, revealing that she wore nothing under her skirt and her t-shirt riding up gave peeks of her aroused breasts. She watched him look at her, and she opened her legs slightly, revealing more. He quickly turned around, disgusted at her open display and crudeness. He knew that Zoe was slightly crazy, but he couldn't leave the house knowing that Zach was left with someone who hated his mother so much. Whether or not Amanda had had a hand in the death of his wife, right now he had to get the information and get Zachary away from here without this crazy woman completely losing it.

"Alex, don't turn away from me now. I want you and you know that you want me. Forget my stupid sister! I am so much better. And... if you please me, I can tell you exactly what happened to Sienna Edwards!" Zoe gave a cackle and sat up, straightening her little outfit. She looked up to see Alex turn to stare at her, hatred stealing its way across his semi-controlled features.

She watched as he controlled his emotions, as he stuffed his hands in his pockets and walked to the other end of the lounge.

"Okay," he said, plonking himself on the armchair close to the television. "Tell me what you know about Sienna and I will make you one happy woman."

Zoe laughed again, staring at him with cats eyes that spelled out danger. "Fine, I'll play your game Mr Edwards. Sienna was my big rescuer. She found me in the warehouse and tried to carry me out. I could feel the fire burning through our clothes and she covered me with her arms, trying to protect me. Do you get the picture of your beloved wife Alex? Covered in flames whilst rescuing a poor child from a burning building? The stupid woman couldn't even carry me the whole way and dropped me down just in front of a gap in the wall. I climbed through safely and collapsed outside. Your dear wife didn't follow."

Zoe looked past Alex, seeing the fire as her face twisted with pain, her hand tracing the burnt stretched skin on the left side of her face. "We both would have been fine if it hadn't been for Amanda. Your wife would be alive today and I would have been ... happy" she whispered, a tear slowing falling down her smooth un-burnt cheek. Her eyes refocused onto Alex. "That's why you should be loving me and not her. You should love my son, not hers!"

With that, Zoe got up and left the room. Alex felt as though he had been punched in the gut. It took a moment for him to catch his breath. Sienna had rescued Zoe from the fire. If she was that close to the warehouse, how did her body turn up in a hit and run in Borrowdale? Why did someone cover up her rescue attempt?

A scream snapped him out of his reverie and he scrambled to his feet, following the terrifying sound filling the air. He ran through a small clean kitchen with black and white tiles on the floor. Through the back

174

stable doors led to a small patio area and sprawling green grass bordered with bright colourful flowers. There, lying on the patio floor was Zachary with Zoe holding a knife to his throat. Kumbi was wrestling with her, their hands entwined around the handle of the knife which precariously wavered closer and closer to the bewildered little boy's throat.

"He will always be mine, just like Jason!" shrieked the she-devil. "I created him. He would never have made a child with that whore sister of mine if I hadn't punctured his supply of condoms. The stupid cheating bastard would have carried on with them both. But ohhh, I knew how much he hated children. He would never stick around if she got pregnant. He would come back to me."

Kumbi twisted her body to the side and used her momentum to hit Zoe, but Zoe blocked her clumsy attack and threw her elbow into Kumbi's ribs, smiling as she heard the woman gasp in pain.

"Maiwe!" screamed Kumbi in shock and pain, as her body crumpled to one side, releasing her feeble grip on Zoe's thin body. As a last ditch attempt, she tried to recover and throw her body between Zach and Zoe. Instead, she ended up landing on Zoe's thin form and grappled with her, trying to grab the knife again. The blade glinted in the sunlight, catching rainbows as it twisted and turned with a deadly shine.

Alex stood paralyzed. Shock at the sight of the two women wrestling, the screaming child cowering in front of them and the full impact of what Zoe was screeching slowly sank in. His body slowly shifted gears until his awareness recovered. He leapt forward, reaching for the hand holding the knife, still trying to pry it out of her surprisingly strong grip. Without hesitation, he punched Zoe in the face with a force he would only use on another man. The knife flipped in the air like a trapeze artist performing a triple spin through the air and landed just in front of Zach's body with a cold silvery clatter.

Zoe lay sprawled out on her back, knocked out by the severe force of Alex's punch. Kumbi had been knocked sideways by the impact, and lay on the ground taking in shaky breaths, whispering incoherent words in her native tongue. Tears stained her dark cheeks. Alex quickly checked Zachary for any injuries and gathered the shivering little body to his, holding him tightly, his own chest rising and falling in gasps, as he sat down hard with the frightened child screaming in his arms.

CHAPTER SIXTEEN

"Call the police Kumbi," Alex instructed the shaking woman. He reached over and shook her shoulder, holding it for a moment, searching her panic stricken eyes to make sure she was okay. "Thank you Kumbi. You saved Zachary's life." She gathered herself up and knelt next to him, her eyes betraying the fear and shock still gripping her.

"Boss, lucky you knew how bad that one was. She is *penga*! Now, Amai will see that for herself," she said. With that, she shrugged her shaking shoulders and staggered up to go make the call.

Alex gently held the quivering child to his body and reached for his own cell phone in his back pocket, searching for David's number and pressing the dial button. Once the police arrived, he would need a friend to clear it up as quickly as possible. Within a few minutes the screaming sirens could be heard approaching the sleepy neighbourhood. They screeched to a halt on the gravel driveway, officers spilling out of hot cars into the humid heat of the November day.

Zoe lay unconscious where she fell from the blow and the paramedics checked her vitals and examined her to assess the damage done by Alex's punch. The police checked the area, and some started taking a statement from Kumbi who had resigned herself to a seat under the avocado tree in the middle of the garden.

David Gallia walked through on his bowed legs, taking in the scene in front of him and made his way to where his tall framed friend stood hunched over, enveloping a little boy who was still crying and shaking in his strong arms. He pulled out his handkerchief out and mopped his bald head, soaking in the dampness that constantly covered his dome in this unrelenting heat. His beady blue eyes turned the minor details he overheard into little snippets of information for the puzzle in his brilliant mind. He assessed the damage before looking at his friend again.

"I guess you got your answers from the sister," he quipped without smiling. "What happened?" he asked as he turned his reddened head to look at the paramedics loading Zoe onto a stretcher and the knife being bagged as evidence by an officer.

Kumbi sat under the shade of the avocado tree in a trance and tears rolled down her dark, freckled cheeks unchecked. The officers taking her statement brought her a cup of water and waited as she sipped it slowly. Alex watched her, as he relayed the story to his friend in a full statement, reliving the events and shuddering inside at the hatred he had encountered.

He had a feeling Zoe had more to do with the fire than she had mentioned. If she had been at the warehouse, maybe she had set the fire, trying to trap Amanda and kill her. Sienna could have caught her and been disposed of to avoid witnesses. The fact that she admitted to tampering with Jason, Amanda and this woman called Lola meant that she would stop at nothing to get what she wanted. She was obsessed with Jason. Amanda's return home with their son must have triggered Zoe's craziness and forced her hand.

David nodded in agreement and huffed. He needed to tie in the fire with Zoe somehow, but the jigsaw pieces still didn't fit right. If Zoe was supposed to be at her friend's and had followed Amanda, could she have knocked Amanda out? Was she the one that set the fire? It would support her severe burns. He looked across at Alex and Zachary and huffed again.

"I need to go back to the office and make a few calls. Will you be okay here?" he asked, taking in the fact that Zachary had not emerged from his cocoon in Alex's arms. "Are you going to tell his mother or shall I go down to the hospital and tell her?"

"No, I'll do it if that's okay Dave. I need to take Zach down to be checked for any injuries and hopefully get them to keep him overnight, so that I can get Amanda to sign a letter saying I can take him home with me.

Otherwise the grandmother is just going to come back and take him again."

"Okay, I'll call you later to check on you." David walked off, stopping to chat to the officer in charge and pointed at Alex, his gestures big on his small frame. The officer nodded and turned to wave at Alex. All clear. He had to get to the hospital before Zoe arrived and tell Amanda what had happened. David would try to contact Esther Munford to inform her on the events of the day. Only more bad could come out of this, and he wanted to get Zachary away as quickly as possible.

 A red truck was parked up on the pavement outside the main gate to 23 Honey Drive and the driver watched the pandemonium, silently watching as the ambulance pulled away from the drive. The man sat still, as Alex reversed his car out of the driveway. He watched Alex thank the police officers for their help and speed off down the road. A little head could be seen in the back seat. The man sighed. Things were getting complicated again. He slowly lit a cigarette and puffed clouds of smoke into the cabin of the truck. The police were slowly leaving the scene and he needed to move before they noticed him there. After another puff, he threw the cigarette out of the open window and cranked the engine which roared to life. Gently manoeuvring the car off the pavement he cruised past the officers chatting outside on the road. He waved at a couple that noticed him and drove off at a

leisurely pace.   He would have to have another chat with
Esther about her family.

The bright sunny afternoon gave way to a wet evening
with hard rain soaking the hot ground. Steam seeped into
the air in wisps. After a couple of hours it subsided and
a blanket of purple Jacaranda flowers coated the roads
and pavements, giving the dark, moonless evening a soft
velvety purple aura. Alex carried a weary little boy up
the last steps to the hospital to where his mother was
waiting, oblivious to the nightmare that had unfolded at
her family home. Amanda smiled with joy when she
saw her two favourite men come towards her but
something in their demeanour warned her that things
were not good. Zachary looked tired and upset. He had
no shoes on, and Alex's set jaw and crazy hair sounded
warning bells in her head.

"What's wrong? What happened?" she asked, afraid of
the answer.

Alex sat heavily in the visitor's chair. Zach seemed like
he was attached to him. He never let go of Alex, as
though his world would end if he did. Amanda's heart
skipped in fear and her mouth went dry. What could
have gone wrong?

"I have something rather distressing to tell you," she heard Alex say, his voice hollow. "I went to see your sister today, to ask her about the fire and the details about what happened. She ... she tried to attack Zachary, Mandy. I don't know what happened. One minute she was telling me about you and her, and your history, and the next, she flipped and went outside to ..." She watched as he gulped for air.

"What?" she asked, unable to comprehend what he was saying.

He stared at her, a different range of emotions playing over his features before he repeated, "Your sister nearly killed your son this afternoon. I'm so sorry Mandy, but I had to knock her out. She is in this hospital under police protection."

Amanda gasped. "What the hell?" She struggled to sit up and groaned in pain. "Tell me everything, NOW!" she screamed.

Her panic made Zach look up. Panic showed across his sweet little face. He started crying, holding on to Alex even tighter.

Amanda couldn't bear it. "Give me my child!" she ordered, trying to keep her hysterical voice down, but Zach refused and clutched tightly to Alex's neck.

"Okay. It's okay Zach. Don't worry, calm down," Alex said, more to Amanda than to the child half choking him. He stroked the little boy's back, waiting until the tears let up a little before speaking again.

"I went to speak to your sister. Remember me mentioning my wife and the way she died? Well somehow she was caught up in the fire at the warehouse and not a hit and run in Borrowdale as reported. I had to find out what Zoe knew about the fire and Sienna's death. She is the only one who doesn't have an alibi for being at the warehouse that night." Alex spoke calmly, afraid the woman before him would react as crazily as her sister. One was enough to deal with in a day and he didn't want Zachary traumatized any more than he was already.

Amanda sensed his trepidation and calmed herself. She nodded, encouraging him to continue.

"I asked her what had happened. She told me that Sienna had rescued her from the fire, but died before she could escape the smoke. That was how she had escaped from the warehouse. Your sister seemed to think it was your fault and held a lot of resentment towards you. She left the room. I heard a scream, which I followed and found her outside holding a knife to Zach's throat."

"She was crazy Amanda. She meddled with Jason's protection ultimately causing your pregnancy. She was following you and knew about your relationship with him. I think that she has an unhealthy obsession with Jason. Anyway, Kumbi and Zoe wrestled for the knife and I knocked her out. They took Zoe away in an ambulance, and she should have arrived here by now," he finished. A stiff drink would cure the dryness scratching away at his throat.

"Oh my God!" was all Amanda could say over and over again. Tears rolled unchecked down her cheeks, and she held her arms out in despair. Alex moved forward with Zach still clinging to him. He hugged them both to him, taking in the wracking sobs from the two people that meant the world to him. He reached up to swipe away the wetness from his own cheeks. It would be okay. Everything had to be okay now.

"Does Ma know what happened?" Amanda asked, still sniffling and rubbing her tired eyes against the roughness of Alex's shirt.

"I don't know. I took Zach to a local doctor to check him over and tried to get him to eat something before we came here." Alex replied. "I have informed the police to notify her, and they will be contacting me to give me an update on any further information they may find."

He hesitated and sat back in the chair, balancing Zachary close to his chest. "Amanda, Zoe was not in her right mind. She spoke to me as clear as day. She hadn't lost her voice, but chose to keep it hidden all this time. I didn't get to find out why. She hates you for always getting the attention and said you had stolen her one true love. Did you know she was in love with Jason?" he asked.

Amanda shook her head. "I knew she looked up to him and used to hang around him all the time, but I didn't think she loved him that way?" She could never imagine her own sister hating her for past boyfriends. Zoe had never let on about her feelings on that score and with the girls drifting apart as they grew older, not much time was spent having heart to heart talks.

"The only two people left who can answer what happened before and after that fateful day are your Gran and Jason. We have to find them and figure out what the hell happened!" Alex said, his face pinched with tension. Amanda nodded in agreement. The time for hiding the truth was over. Lives were at risk, and if they didn't figure out this mess soon, someone else could get hurt, like Esther. She seemed to be in the dark about most of Zoe's true personality and obviously Jason had to know Zoe better than he claimed to since he was her lover!

CHAPTER SEVENTEEN

The red truck pulled up outside Beker's Bakery in Avondale. It had served as a delivery vehicle for the past two years, and still had a glossy shine to its paintwork, as did the owner who stepped out into the twighlight filled with glittering raindrops that had fallen a few minutes before. His balding head reflected the delicate drops hanging from the car roof as he locked his door and made his way to the bakery entrance. The man had a regal posture and a definite, firm stride as he walked into the bakery. His smart brown suit covered a rather dashing figure for an older man, and his ready smile softened the deep frown lines just above his thick bushy eyebrows.

The bell above the door tinkled and a pair of hazel eyes looked up from behind the counter to watch the approaching figure. They twinkled with delight and slight creases appeared on either side of a pretty mouth that still held a hint of the beautiful youth trapped in an older woman's body.

Esther watched as her long-time lover, Alfred Beker walked towards her with his regal gait. She had loved this man for many years, and had watched him grow old gracefully, with the clarity of purpose she found in few people around her. Her smile slipped slightly when she observed his stern expression. There were few times that Alfred didn't smile. When they told him he had to leave his family home to join the army; when his wife died; when he found out that the love of his life had married; and when his daughter had died. The same expression darkened his face now, and a determined thrust of his jaw elongated his features.

"What's wrong my love?" asked Esther, concerned that something terrible had happened. She wiped her hands and walked around the counter. Alfred stopped in front of her and gathered her hands into his own. His expression softened slightly as he noticed how concerned she looked.

"I have gone to your house Es and something happened," he said slowly, his thick accent enunciating the words heavily. "Zoe was involved in an incident with that man you told me about. He came to the house asking questions about the fire and she tried to attack the child. He hit her, and she had to go to hospital." The sing song quality of his voice lilted through his telling of the tale and Esther's face grew pale and gaunt. Her eyes were as big as saucers and filled with unshed tears.

"You have to help me Alfie" she cried. "You have to help me end this madness!"

"I know. I know my love," he replied in his slow drawl. Alfred's shoulders dropped under the pressure of feeling responsible for this wonderful woman in front of him.

187

He knew what he had to do – protect the one he loved more than anything else in this world. With a gentle pat on her hands, he led the way to the back rooms of the bakery. They sat down together, thoughts heavily weighed by the knowledge that they couldn't protect Zoe anymore.

In the meantime, Alex, Amanda, and Zachary made their way out of the hospital car park to Alex's car and drove the few kilometres back to their temporary home in Avondale, just behind the shopping centre. Amanda could feel the strain of travelling in a car again and tried her best not to flinch at approaching traffic, or a car horn beeping at the early evening traffic. A cold sweat broke out across her top lip, as she clung to the door handle, holding her breath at every turn.

At last the little side road to the house appeared, and she relaxed knowing the trip was over. Her right arm was still in a sling and though her pounding headache resonated through any sound higher than a few decibels, she was happy to be out of the hospital and back in normal surroundings with Alex and Zachary.

Once the car was parked safely close to the kitchen, Alex nimbly leapt out. He opened her door and Zachary's, lending a supporting hand for her to lean on, as she cautiously made her way up the step into the kitchen. A fresh bunch of wild flowers were arranged in a beautiful crystal cut vase and a big card with teddies on the front beckoned to her with a sign, "Welcome Home!" plastered across it.

She grinned with delight and squeezed Alex's arm at the wonderful surprise. His dark eyes lit with warmth that resonated through her body leaving her tingly all over. There was a surprise for Zachary too – a big teddy bear with soft fur to cuddle, which he didn't hesitate trying out. He still held one hand close to Alex, who he hadn't left alone since being rescued from his great-grandmother's house. The teddy was clasped close to his chest, and he nuzzled the bear's soft ears, whispering sweet sentiments that only the bear could hear.

Amanda mouthed a thank you above her traumatized child's head, as they continued into the lounge where she slowly sat down, feeling drained from all the exertion. Alex watched her progress with a worried expression wrinkling his strong brow.

"Do you need your painkillers Mandy?" he asked, his deep voice resonating concern.

"No, I'm fine thank you. The car trip rattled me a little but I will be okay thanks." She smiled up at his worried face, wondering how lucky she could be to have a man so strong and kind looking after her. Amanda realised that they needed to talk about the future, and whether it held a possibility of them being together. Could he

189

forgive her for having such a crazy family? If it was true that his wife was somehow involved in the fire many years ago, would he be able to look past that too? As though reading her mind, Alex drew closer and gave her free hand a gentle squeeze.

"We'll talk soon. Right now I have to make a few calls and find out if your grandmother has been found and notified about Zoe." His face turned grim again.

"Okay" Amanda replied, tired and already curling up on the sofa. "I'll be here if you need me," she mumbled, closing her eyes as the last word filtered out.

Alex gathered Zach and his toys, taking them with him to the dining room, which also acted as an office. Once Zach was settled he made his call to David Gallia. After two rings David picked up and greeted Alex. His usual upbeat manner seemed subdued. Alex knew that something was wrong.

"Alex, I have some rather disturbing news about Amanda Glenson's accident. We have the preliminary report, and it seems that the brakes on her car were tampered with. It would explain why she couldn't stop at the intersection," David sighed into the phone, wishing he could give his friend some good news for a change.

"Whoever tampered with the brakes wanted to get rid of Amanda and the child. The only person I can think of is her sister, based on the attack the other day. If that is the case, we can close this matter, as the sister is going to be charged with assault on a minor and probably found to be insane."

Alex could hear the 'but' before David said it and voiced his friend's concern. "You think that maybe Zoe wasn't working alone!"

"Uh-huh!" David exclaimed. "There are too many loose ends in this case and the cold case too. How could Zoe get rid of your wife's body if she was in hospital with major burns? Even if she set the fire, I don't think she was so masochistic to stay in harm's way once her sister was trapped. I think getting burnt was an accident she, or whoever helped her couldn't foresee. They had to get rid of your wife, as a witness, and there is another problem too."

"What is it?" Alex asked.

"Well, to fudge a police report at a crime scene would need some serious clout. Getting rid of a body and filing it under a different case... well, we are talking heavy artillery if you know what I mean, my friend," chuckled David.

Alex sighed. He knew what his friend meant. This was the reason why he could never get any further in his investigation into his wife's death. Someone in the police force was helping Zoe. They had covered up the evidence of Sienna's involvement as well, as making the evidence point to Amanda as the culprit. A person with that much power would have to be a highly ranked officer. But why? All the pieces didn't seem to fit. They knew Zoe's hatred of Amanda had drawn her out to show her hand, but whoever had assisted in the crimes was still at large, and probably close by.

Alex clutched the phone tightly. "David, have you checked out Jason Florentine yet? He has been involved with the family from the start and may have the biggest motive out of them all. From what I have noticed, he seems pretty well connected to different people through his business transactions. Also, we don't know anything about his family other than they are successful entrepreneurs."

"How so?" David's said intrigued at a new possibility.

"Jason has been involved with both Zoe and Amanda. He is the father of Amanda's child and has been supporting the family for I don't know how long." Alex felt a cold ripple go down his back. "Would he hate Amanda enough to try and get rid of her and the child, so that he could be free to be with Zoe?"

"I don't know, but we will definitely investigate that avenue," replied David. "In the meantime, I think it would be best if you kept them both close to you in case he tries again. I am going to dig deeper into the family history too, just to make sure we haven't missed another wannabe culprit." he continued. "Be careful, Alex. Whoever is doing this is not playing games anymore."

Alex thanked his friend and cut the call. Zachary was staring at him with a very serious expression. "Who is coming to hurt us Alex?" he asked, his little voice sounding very mature. Alex sighed with resignation and slid off his chair to join Zachary on the floor amongst his toys.

"I'm not sure kid. All I know is there are people out there who feel they need to hurt your mommy. I will do my best to protect both of you," he said, touching Zach's nose with his index finger. "But my friend is a policeman who will help us fix things and arrest these bad people, okay? That's who I was talking to on the phone. I want you to know that nothing is going to hurt you Zach. You're safe here. Okay buddy?"

Zachary sat in silence for a few seconds, absorbing the information he was given and then looked up at Alex and smiled. "I knew you would take care of Mummy and me!" he said, leaping into Alex's waiting arms for a big hug. Yep, maybe things would be okay after all.

CHAPTER EIGHTEEN

Smoke has filled the room, making it hard to see and even harder to breathe. Someone was coughing and choking in another part of the house, but there was no clear sight to see which way to go. Lights were flickering on and off, as though it was a disco. A loud pop followed by crackling sounds made my hair stand on end. Fire!

I have to get off this bed, even though the blankets feel like dead weight pressing down on my chest, holding me underwater. I feel like I'm drowning in white clouds. Coughing and trying to wrap part of the sheet across my face, I roll and hit the ground hard, the weight of my body knocking the air out of my lungs. Precious air that caused near choking suffocation when I tried to retrieve it.

Crawling slowly, I feel for the dark objects that tend to rise up and bash into my head out of the dark! I'm crawling across the floor, and I can just make out the door in the dim flickering light, which is getting closer. The heat burns at my eyebrows, and I can feel my arms scorching but there is no flame to be seen as yet, thank God. A little voice is clearly screaming now in fear. I know who it is. My heart is a piece of lead melting with a sickening feeling. I need to focus on getting there first.

In the passageway between the rooms, the inferno rears its ugly head. I can see the fury of the flames licking their way up the walls and tearing the ceiling apart with ferocity. Bits of plaster float down within a dangerous proximity to my clothing. Everything else that isn't burning watches enthusiastically, as the sparks flitter through the air to light them up in glory. I am getting closer to Zach's room, and I can just barely push the door open. Good! The room hasn't filled with that much smoke, as I crawl towards his bed, where he is sitting up crying and screaming.

A cough attack stops the caterwauling. I use the opportunity to pull him down next to me, covering his face with my sheet. Ah, a glass of water on his bedside table provides ample dampness to filter the hot scalding air around us. Time to move on.

"Come on! You have to be brave and stay with me. Okay?" I scream, not realising until then just how loud a fire can be. Another pop and a loud boom make us both hug each other in fear. His big brown eyes look at me with complete fear and something I didn't expect, trust. I know I have to fight to save us both. We can't give up. "Let's go!" I shout to him, and we turn in unison, crawling like soldiers across the floor to the door again.

Back into the passageway the flames are so close my toes are starting to barbeque! I push Zach in front of me, away from the tongues of fire trying to burn off skin, as we battle to open the last door. It's locked! Shit! I have to stand to kick the door in, but my muscles refuse to oblige. Big knots have formed in my gluts and thighs and it takes maximum effort to lift myself off the ground for the full momentum of a hearty kick to break down Amanda's door. Why the hell would she have locked her door? I collapse as I gratefully see the hinges give way with a crack, and we push through, shuffling past the broken shards of wood. Zach crouches forward and grabs my arm, pulling me with all his might and screaming something incoherent.

I must have passed out, as the house is on fire around us. A sooty black face is looking at me, and I recognise the brown eyes, filled with tears and fear. Shaking my cotton wool head with the makings of a mother migraine, I try to decipher where I am. I'm still in the passageway and my trousers are burning! Slapping my legs to kill the flames just helps the material stick to my burning skin.

A little hand is pulling me again. I use what little energy I've gathered to pull myself forward into Amanda's room. She is barely visible. I can just make out the figure of her body slumped against the white sideboard, like a discarded ragdoll thrown into the corner of the room. The only coherent sound is my heart doing its panicky triple beat, as I look for tell-tale signs of self-harm. Could she be...?

No. I pull Zachary back, as he tries to get up and run to her. Wrapping his face in the sheet again we move forward at a steady pace, our hearts racing ahead to her. She is cold to the touch and her pulse is thready. There is a pool of blood trickling down the side of her head. She is so pale. I can feel Zachary shaking next to me, and I quickly hug him to me, trying to find words of comfort, but nothing escapes from my dried crusty mouth. Not that he would hear me anyway above the noise.

We have to escape. The windows are all burglar barred and locked. The bathroom in my bedroom was the only window without burglar bars. You have got to love a country that protects its residents from thugs and murderers, but not household fires! If I could reach my room with them both, they could escape through the small glazed window without a problem. Just a small distance through hell, that's all. I'm sure it could fit a big man like me without a problem. Looking over at Zachary I can tell that he won't last for much longer. I have to make the hard decision.

"Zachary! We're going to leave your mum to sleep for a while and I'm going to take you outside where it's safe okay? I'll come back for her, but I need you to be brave for me for a little while longer. Can you do that for me?" My chest hurts from screaming out instructions to a little five year old who stares into my eyes with his innocence, and trusts me implicitly, without question.

Let's hope I don't disappoint. Gently kissing his mother he crawls back to me, and holds my arm tight. I hug him to me again, and we make our move.

Getting to my bedroom and into the bathroom is taking longer than anticipated, and by the time Zachary is halfway out of the window, I'm ready to pass out again. The heat overwhelms the senses, and the smoke consumes my lungs leaving me feeling the burn throughout my body, like an ashtray with cigarette butts being put out in it. Suddenly, a pair of large hands reach in and grab Zachary from me. Panicking, I try to grab him back, succeeding in ripping the skin from my forearm and causing a bitch of pain to spread up my already burning arm.

"I got him! Where's Amanda?" a voice screams down a tunnel at me. "Can you hear me? Where's Amanda?"

Tunnel voice is shouting so loud now, I can hear it clearly again, and shout back that she's hurt. I'm going back to get her now. My voice is croaky and barely carries through the noise. I don't wait for a response. The crawl back to her is long and laborious, but I know that she needs me. The fresh air from the bathroom window has a refreshing effect on tired burnt lungs and skin. I move slightly faster, trying to ignore the coughing fits that try to slow my progress.

Clarity is my companion, as I realise that my world exists around this woman and her little boy. Forget about my doubts and the glaring possibility she might...no, she is involved in a similar situation that killed my wife. Amanda is the beacon I want to come home to everyday, and the thought of losing her is making my chest hurt more, if that is physically possible.

New energy surges through my body and my adrenaline kicks me forward, crawling faster through the already half charred passageway. I look into the smoky distance and see that most of the lounge and kitchen are missing, leaving weird open gaps where walls and doors should have been. Weird red and blue orbs circle in the distance and figures can just be made out in the gaps.

No time to waste. Amanda is slung over my shoulder. Was she always this fragile? She feels like a light load of beautiful swan, flailing in a wispy body. Her limp body worries me, but I don't have the luxury of checking her pulse again. The room is on fire, and the bed is a raging inferno, adding unwanted heat to an already frustrating situation.

The wetness I showered over myself in my en-suite is a wish away from dryness, and I throw another cup of water over both of us from the carafé on the chest of drawers. We reach the bathroom in time to shut the door on an exploding pillow from my charred bed. Hands reach in again to help lift her gently over the window sill and she disappears into the darkness. I climb out after her, gasping in pain, as my body distorts into shapes a man my size should never hope to achieve.

The ground kisses my body with aching bruises, and I look up to find a man staring at me with what looks like relief in his eyes. I take the arm offered and pull myself up, folding over again, as a coughing attack seizes me. With eyes watering and a burning, retching feeling enveloping my throat, I don't have time to thank him before he walks off to assist the fire fighters who had arrived at the scene God knows when. Jason's profile is highlighted by the flames as he walks away from me, leaving me to question what the hell he is doing here.

Amanda opened her eyes to a brilliant sunny day with the birds singing outside her window, as a gentle breeze blowing the curtains in a seductive dance. She stretched out her arms and yawned, feeling the sleepiness shrug off her body, as a lovely tug of hunger made her tummy rumble. Hmm, thought Amanda, some breakfast and maybe a long hot shower, and then up to wash her hair.

She picked at strands of her long wavy brown curls and sniffed them. Definitely a shower! Her hair smelt like burnt cat. Not that she'd ever smelt a burnt cat, but she could imagine it wouldn't smell much worse than her hair. Suddenly, the curl withered in her hand and turned to ash, as did the other curls. She spotted her reflection in the mirror opposite the bed and watched as her hair disappeared in a puff of ash and smoke. She screamed, as the rest of her head caught fire. She watched in terror and fascination, as the flames licked away at her bald scalp. Panic filled every pore and drowned out her shrieks whilst the fire swallowed her nightdress, engulfing her body.

Hands shook her awake, and she looked up to find Jason gently stroking her wild untamed hair out of her face. Every hair, was still intact and un-burnt.

"What the hell? Where am I?" she gasped, pushing his hands away as the panic and fear held her in its deathly grip. Her arm was in a cast and she could feel a bandage wrapped around her forehead like a bandana.

"Don't worry, you're okay!" he smiled, grasping her flailing limbs. "Calm down! I promise I won't hurt you Bumblebee. I'm so sorry I ever caused you this much pain. Please trust me again!" His eyes shone with tears and his humbled expression was so uncharacteristic, Amanda stopped and stared at him.

"Okay," she gulped. "Tell me where I am and why you are here Jason?" she asked again, heart thumping, as she forced her voice to stay at a level tone.

"This man is a hero!" came a reply from the other side of her bed. She jumped and turned to see a tall thin man in a doctor's coat standing next to her. "I'm Doctor Chikori. You are back in hospital after escaping a fire at your house. This man helped to rescue you and your family from certain death," he said with great relish, smiling with huge corn yellow teeth.

"My son, Zachary. Is he okay?" she shivered, trying to piece together missing memories.

"Yes. Yes. He is fine thanks again to this man. He pulled your son out and delivered him to the hospital in time to make sure his lungs were cleared of any smoke inhalation. Your son is playing in the rest room next door. I will leave you now with your hero and go see to my other patients." He walked out with his disturbingly large grin, with his white coat flapping behind him.

Jason smiled at Amanda's bewildered face.

"I know it seems confusing now, but there was a fire at your house. I got there just in time to get you guys out, but the house is a mess. Some of your documents have been retrieved, but most of the items in the house are destroyed. Sorry Bumblebee," he commiserated, softly rubbing her cold hand.

"Umm, thank you Jason," she replied. "But, what were you doing at my house?"

A glaze passed over his face trying to mask the hurt and pain hidden in its depths and yes, a hint of anger at being doubted by her.

"I came to apologise to you again for messing around with Zoe. I knew she was in a vulnerable state, but she came on so strong, and I missed you so much. She was always there, comforting me and needing someone to look after her. I guess I took advantage of the situation with her and now I feel responsible. I came to tell you that and saw the fire. I called the police and the fire brigade, but managed to help you escape before it was too late."

"What about Alex? Is he okay? Was he hurt?" she asked, worry filling her voice.

"Nah, he's fine. He got a couple of cuts and burns, but he'll be okay. They're just keeping a check on his chest because he inhaled a lot of smoke." Jason leaned forward, closer to her. She could pick out the little gold flecks in his brown eyes. Sincerity screamed from his every pore, as she caught a glimpse of the man she had once called her best friend. A man she had trusted enough to share her first sexual experience.

"Mandy, I'm sorry I mistook your relationship with your co-worker or boss for something else. I was insanely jealous. Which, I know gave me no excuse for attacking you. I've said some really hurtful things about our son too, and this fire has made me realise what I could have lost."

Jason released her hand and wiped his face that had grown wet. His chest heaved, and Amanda felt a pang of compassion for a man who was trying to settle so many wrongs from his past. She reached forward and stroked his wet cheek with her left hand, her right tied close to her chest to protect her shoulder.

"I know. I'm sorry too. I should have contacted you and told you that you were a father. I had no right keeping it from you. It's just that I was so afraid. Afraid of coming home and facing a bleak future of always having that doubt placed on me whether I set the fire at Dad's warehouse, or not. I knew you would have moved on, and I didn't want to be the black sheep of the family, gossip feeding off our son!"

"Never Amanda!" he said, his face serious with love pouring from his wide brown eyes. "I could never move on knowing that you could come home. That's why I stepped in to help your Dad when the insurance didn't pay out. I would never leave your family to face financial ruin. It was Esther that suffered the most. She had tried so hard to come back into the circle and when you left, your mum and dad were devastated. She stepped in and held the family together, but it took a lot out of her. She looked after Zoe when she came back from the hospital and helped her recover from her injuries.'

'I could only offer my support with money and they kindly offered me a place to stay when I needed to move out from my parent's house." Jason sighed and ran a heavy hand through his brown curls. "I would do it all again for you my Bumblebee. Everything I do is for you. I want to be with you. I love Zachary. He is my son, and he needs a daddy. Do you think you could ever forgive me and maybe look at staying so that we can have a chance of keeping the family together?"

Amanda stared at Jason. She was trying to make sense of a world that had crumbled around her, and now he was offering a future for her and Zachary. She understood the dangers of being with a man like Jason. He was arrogant, and he had done so much wrong with her and Zoe. There was a chance he could hurt her physically and the fear of his anger lingered, as well as the doubts about his involvement with Zoe. But he was Zach's father and he had kept her family together when she had run away. Didn't she owe him just a little forgiveness? Didn't he have the right to be angry with her lies?

But what about Alex? She knew that he was the one she loved and the thought of losing him made her shiver. A world without him by her side, making her smile and loving him when he played with her son. Did she love him because he accepted Zachary and was willing to love them both? He was the first man she had allowed to penetrate her family circle and now it was time to decide whether she loved him for accepting Zach, or because she was crazy about him for herself.

"Jason, I can't give you an answer now. I need time. There are too many things I need to sort out in my life first and until I can do that, I don't know what I'm going to do."

Jason nodded in understanding and got up, giving her a lingering kiss on her lips. "Just remember that I will always be waiting for you my little Bumblebee," he whispered against her mouth, kissing her again.

He left, leaving her emotions in turmoil.

Alex watched the scene unfold before him and turned away, as Amanda returned Jason's kiss. His heart fell through an already heavy chest. As he slowly returned to the rest room to play with Zach, he knew that his time with this little guy was limited. He was kidding himself all along that he could adopt an instant family. As he sat down, Zachary ran to give him another hug and started another long tale about his toys, whilst Alex smiled and laughed at the appropriate times. Soon it would be time for him to go home, and he had to make the difficult decision for both himself and Amanda.

Things were dangerous, and the more they dug into their pasts, it seemed to encourage the violence that followed. This fire could have been set by Amanda, or maybe, Jason had come to help her. He shook his head to clear it and scratched at the long wavy curls at the base of his skull.

Confusion hit him hard, and he realised that his love for Amanda had clouded his judgement. Her whole family was a mess, and the closer he got, the more he would get hurt. It wouldn't be easy leaving before finding out the full details of how Sienna died, but it was time for him to stop pursuing it and let Amanda follow her family and apparently, her heart.

A week in hospital gave the three victims enough time to recuperate and it gave Mr Ismail, the local lawyer who had been assisting them in their business transactions, time to sort out fresh documentation, hotel accommodations, and clothing for the three of them. He kindly visited them in hospital and made sure that they wanted for nothing.

Jennifer Cook, Amanda's boss back in England, was kept up to date on what had transpired over the past weeks and sent back instructions for them to return once they were in good enough health to travel. The business side of Alex and Amanda's trip was over, but the loose ends from their past still hung like ribbons trailing in the wind.

David Gallia followed the investigation into the fire and found accelerants were used to start it. Fingerprints were lifted from Amanda's room, and he started putting the pieces together that would give them a better picture of who was behind the misfortune that had followed the Glenson family and killed so many of its members.

Gallia kept his findings to himself, as he trusted few people in the corrupt police department where he knew pay-offs could throw all the evidence back under the carpet. He was so close, really close to putting the last jigsaw piece in place. He had to wait patiently, because he knew that person would try one last time to end the actions started five years before. David was good at waiting and even better at investigating. Add to that the emotional turmoil of having his friend slap bang in the middle of this mess, and David had to be at the top of his game.

CHAPTER NINETEEN

Meikles Hotel welcomed back their bedraggled guests and made them feel at home again. Amanda and Alex felt relieved to be cleared from the hospital and back into their own private space. Christmas had taken over the shopping centres and Unity Square sported old fashioned Christmas lights with big colourful bulbs twinkling and flickering in the evening sky, competing with cars' tail lights flashing on and off as shoppers enjoyed the late night shopping hours in the nearby mall.

Thunder rumbled in the distance, but stars twinkled overhead, and the warmth of the day was replaced with a coolness that was fresh and pleasant. Zachary had crashed out earlier in the evening and now that they were sharing a suite, he seemed more settled having Alex around. He was still nervous on his own and felt a sense of security with this man he had come to look at as a father-figure in his life. Amanda felt her own relief having Alex close to her, and she relied on him to help with the caring of Zach as her shoulder and arm hurt more than she cared to admit.

Alex turned from the window, a crease forming above his brow, as he tried to figure out how to broach the subject of their relationship. He felt cold hands envelope him in a tight hug as Amanda caressed his chest with small butterfly movements and lay her head against his back, drawing the warmth he naturally exuded from his tall frame that had thinned out and bore the scars and burns of the fire. Sighing contentedly, she felt the rhythm of his heart beating against her ear. He gently removed her hands and turned to her, stroking her cheek and smiling.

"Mandy, we have to talk. So much has happened and I need to clear the air about a few things that just can't wait anymore." He stepped back and dropped his hands to his side, trying to gauge her reaction.

She sighed again, flicking her beautiful long brown curls out of her eyes, pulling it back where it bounced around her head, as soon as she released it, creating a golden halo. She looked ethereal, soft, and fragile. He wanted to sweep her back into his arms and blot out the rest of the world. He knew he couldn't. Too much stood between them and their future and the way things were heading, it looked as though she had settled on staying with him. Did he want that? He had to find out.

"Where shall we start Alex?" she replied, choosing to sit in a comfortable chair on the other side of the room. She curled her long legs under her, and wrapped her hands around the stripped scatter cushion that had been lying on the chair.

"I need to know your involvement in the fire, once and for all Mandy. Did you start the fire?" he asked, the knowledge of what he was doing turning his face sombre and his eyes an even darker black than normal. His overgrown raven-coloured hair had fallen forward, nearly covering his eyebrows, which gave him the look of a dangerous pirate. "The only reason I need to ask this question is to clear the air about how my wife died. I know that she was there, and I can piece together why, but who would want to hurt her? Who would leave her to die in a fire where she was trying to rescue the victims?" he sighed, despair overtaking all his other emotions.

Amanda watched him and swallowed the hurt and anger she felt. They had to be honest again with each other and she understood that though they had discussed this before, he needed confirmation to assuage his doubts.

"I don't know about your wife Alex. I wasn't even aware that she was there. Even Zoe being there was a surprise. I thought my sister was safe and sound at her friend's house. I never dreamt that she had been injured in the fire. When I woke up and found I was surrounded by smoke and flames, I panicked, screaming for my Dad who was supposed to be in the offices. I tried the phone, but it was dead. I assumed the fire had burnt the wires, so I ran out as fast as I could to reach a phone and get help. That's the truth Alex. I never saw anyone." She ran her hand through her wayward hair again, stirring up the halo and making it fall softly around her face. The soft light emanating from the table lamp next to the double bed cast shadows along the walls. Amanda's shadow danced and flickered as her hair fell back into place.

"Okay, so you didn't start the fire. Someone else did then, maybe Zoe. But, if Zoe was the one who knocked you out and tried to escape the fire, why did Sienna enter a burning building that should have been empty at that time of night? Unless someone screamed to alert her whilst she was jogging. Could you have screamed when you were knocked out or when you woke up?" he asked, anxiously leaning forward from his seat on the end of the bed. Amanda watched his shadow stretch up along the wall to the ceiling. It resembled a monster. She shuddered.

"No! I only remember the darkness enveloping me. I was so upset about Jason, and how he had lied to me about our relationship. The pregnancy and his announcement of his engagement filled my thoughts. That was what was on my mind. I was worried about my Dad too. He had been under a lot of pressure before the fire because his business was not doing well. That's what pushed me to go find him. I didn't know how stable he was, and needed to talk to him. He loved to talk to me, when he wasn't criticizing my poor decisions! Who knew that he would be right about Jason!" she sighed, closing her eyes and reminiscing over her past.

"Wait a minute! What was that about your dad and Jason?" Alex asked, springing up from his despondent position. "I thought Jason was the son he never had, the saviour of his business after the fire?"

"Yes! I don't understand that either," she replied, straightening up, as thoughts began to gel. "He always hated me befriending Jason and warned me often, saying he was not a good guy. When he found out that I was secretly hanging out with him, he was livid and screamed at me. He was so disappointed in me. Jason would have been the last person my father would do business with. Why didn't I think of that before?" she frowned, angry with herself. Talking about it with Alex seemed to pull the pieces of her history together. She had buried it so deep to avoid the pain of the memories.

"What else do you remember Amanda?" he asked. "This could be important!"

She frowned, trying to dredge through happy and unhappy memories of her teenage years.

"I remember entering the warehouse and the lights were on. There was a noise upstairs, and that is what made me check the offices to see if Dad was still working."

"Did anyone else apart from Jason know that you were going there?" Alex asked, his frown creasing his forehead again. The muscle in his jaw jumped as he bit down, his feet soundlessly pacing up and down on the soft thick carpet.

"Only the person that made the anonymous call to me. Could that have been Zoe?" she gasped, holding a hand to her mouth, as she realised just how much her sister could have been involved in trying to hurt her.

"Maybe. We can't ask her until she is found. Her disappearance from the hospital was a bit too convenient and easy considering she was under police guard at the time. I can't believe we missed her by a day. If we had gone to see her the day before yesterday, maybe we would have had the answers we need to solve this mystery. Once we find her we will have to ask her, but if your dad was against your relationship with Jason and if Jason knew how much your dad hated him, he could have set the fire. There was no stopping him from following you to the warehouse and setting it. He could have been working with Zoe all along, using his break-up with you and a false engagement to Lola as his alibi for not being there. He could have been the one who killed my wife!" Alex said, stopping in mid-pace and facing Amanda's curled up figure on the chair.

"But why? I mean he saved my father's business after all, and has been helping my family since my parents' deaths," she said, picking at little cotton strings dangling from the striped cushion. "What motive would he have for helping my family if he was out to destroy them?"

"I don't know Mands. I don't know." Alex raked his hand through his hair sending it flying backwards. "He had the strength to move Sienna's body and an alibi for not being around. He had ample opportunity to tamper with your brakes too, and he had the working knowledge of how to do it. Whereas your Gran, as somewhat guilty as she seems, would never try to hurt you. I don't think Zoe would have been capable of tampering with your brakes either."

"But he would never hurt his own son. He told me that he loves him and wants to be a part of his life Alex. I can't believe that Jason would do something so stupid as to risk the life of his son whilst trying to hurt me," she replied angrily.

"You don't understand Amanda. Your own sister admitted that Jason hates children and didn't want any of his own. Why would he suddenly start caring when he hasn't shown an ounce of fatherly love towards your son since you told him he's the father?" Alex retorted, his own anger rising at her defence of Jason.

"That's because I never gave him a chance to get to know his own son. I was too busy playing happy families with you!" Amanda shouted back, rising from her chair and dropping the cushion on the floor in the process. "If I hadn't been so worried about you and your reactions, maybe I would have given the father of my child a better chance of getting to know his own son!"

Alex face turned a stony grey, and his hands clenched at his sides. His eyes glowered, as he straightened himself to his full height, towering above Amanda. "If I hadn't stepped in to look after your son, he would be dead now thanks to your crazy family. I didn't need you or your troubles at my door, but here you are! Somehow our history is intertwined and I'm still trying to establish whether or not you're just as crazy as the rest of your family! Maybe you are the missing link in the murder of my wife and until I find out the truth, I am not going to back down!" he growled, edging towards her.

She watched him approach, fear stealing across her angry features and she took a step back, her legs colliding with the chair behind her. Her reaction sobered Alex instantly and his heart sank, as he watched the woman he loved so much cower in front of him, afraid of his anger. He quickly unclenched his fists and took a step back towards the bed, noticing her drop her own clenched hand and recover her composure.

"Amanda, I would never hurt you. You know that, don't you?" he asked. "Has your life always been surrounded by violence? Is that why you react to me this way?" he asked from the safe distance of the double bed. He needed to hold her, to reassure her that he was not like the other men in her life.

Amanda sighed. She shakily wiped a film of cold sweat that had appeared above her brow. "I don't know. It's just that my Dad, Jason, and everyone I've ever known, seem to have a handle on their emotions. I guess it's just instinct to flinch. I am not afraid of you, and I know you won't hurt me. But, we are both riding this emotional roller coaster, and I can't seem to convince you that I had nothing to do with your wife's death. I realise that I'm not sure how you react when angry. I don't know you that well Alex." Tears welled up, and she brushed them aside.

"No, please don't cry Mandy," he sighed, slowly moving forward until he could kneel in front of her. He gently stroked her wet cheeks. "I would never hurt you. I could never hurt you. I love you too much. But you must understand that I need to know about your past…what happened to my wife? I hate the way you defend that asshole. That makes me angry, but never angry enough to hurt you. Please, trust me," he said, gently kissing her and feeling her trembling body.

"I know you won't, but I still feel scared. I haven't been near a man since Jason, and it's a new experience having someone else to rely on, to fight with, who doesn't throw blows when he's angry," she smiled nervously.

"Okay, look we have to get to the bottom of both the fires and your accident. We know that Jason is involved somehow, but we have to find out why he helped your family all these years. What was his motive and why would he try to hurt you now?" Alex said, holding onto Amanda until her shaking subsided.

"Alex, you have to understand that I've thought about Jason as a dad for Zachary. He saved us from the house fire and he was there to make sure we were okay in the hospital. Even after my car accident, he has been there." She looked at Alex's cold expression and continued before her courage failed her.

"I know that we just threw angry words around but there is a truth in what we have said. I haven't given him a chance to be a dad and yes you have stepped up. Maybe we are finding a scape-goat in Jason. I'll be the first to admit he has a bit of a temper and can throw a punch, but I don't think he means to hurt me, or Zach." There. She said it and breathed out in relief. At least she was being honest with the man she loved and could try to move forward.

Alex watched the woman he loved. The soft light caught the dark smudges under her eyes, the loving eyes that begged for trust. A plan formed in his mind and he decided to take the risk, just as she had and tell her the plan.

 "I need to ask you to do something that might put you at risk. It will help us get to the bottom of all of this once and for all. Do you think you can do it?" he asked, kissing her gently on her cheek.

"Hmm. Okay," she whispered, trying to concentrate on his words and not his lips that were playing havoc with her emotions. "What do you need me to do?"

CHAPTER TWENTY

The car idled gently under me as I waited for the gate to open. Kumbi half smiled at me when she checked to see who was in the unrecognisable grey Nissan Almera and promptly opened the gate wider, so that I could drive through. The stones gave a familiar crunch under the cars' wheels and I turned the steering wheel, following the driveway to park under the big jacaranda tree at the end of the drive. The criss-cross pattern of leaves and branches reflected off the windshield, allowing slivers of bright blue to shine through. I was grateful for my sunglasses, as I moved away from the car and stood in the sun which hit me square in the eye, nearly blinding my sight.

I put my hand over my glasses to try to glimpse if anyone would come out of the house to greet me. Jason's pick up was parked in the car port to the right of the front door, just beyond the rose bushes. A red pickup truck I didn't recognise stood cosily in the space next to Jason's pick up. Maybe they had visitors and I was imposing. No! This used to be my home too and I had more right to be here than Jason. Picking my way carefully over the jagged stones, I walked the path, taking in the lovely soft scent of the pink and red roses. As I approached the veranda the front door opened and Ma came out to greet me.

She hugged me tight, tighter than she had hugged me before, and the sadness in her eyes made mine water. I hadn't seen her since Zoe's disappearance from the hospital and her few visits and numerous apologies for Zach's ill treatment under her care. She was looking thinner and so fragile. Her hazel eyes danced with tears. She rubbed her thin long fingers against my upper arms.

"I never thought you would come back to see me Ma. Not after everything that's happened. How's my baby, Zach?" she enquired, hope making her glance back to the car parked under the jacaranda tree. I shook my head to confirm he wasn't with me. I couldn't bring myself to tell her that I would never bring Zach close to her after what she did to him and allowed Zoe to do to him in her care.

"I came back to say good-bye Ma," I replied. "We are leaving the day after tomorrow to get back before Christmas. I just wanted to come and see you to make sure that I can clear the air between us." I looked her in the eye, hoping to see forgiveness for Zoe's injuries and her consequent disappearance from hospital before being charged with assault on a minor, which I felt was my fault; as were all the other things that had happened in the past. Only sorrow reflected outward, and I felt so lonely; my only family separated from me through the horrible circumstances that seemed to follow us like death's servant.

"Come inside Ma." She took my hand and drew me into the house. "I want you to meet my very special friend, Alfie. He is the one that keeps me strong and has always been there for me." She smiled a genuine smile, her eyes a sparkling green, while radiating a joy only love could create. I smiled in return, happy to see that my grandmother had someone to hold her together through all of the turmoil.

I was greeted by a bear hug that nearly squeezed my poor shoulder out of its setting and made my tender arm ache. The bald man in front of me was average in height and rather handsome for his age. His eyes sparkled with delight. He exuded charm, as he spoke with an eloquence of a colonial teacher. I felt as if I had met him before, his smile was familiar.

"What a beautiful grand-daughter you have here Es! I'm not surprised you've kept her hidden away. She is the spitting image of you when you were younger," he laughed, squeezing my hand warmly. "Come join us outside in the garden. It is far too stuffy to stay in the house," he said, leading the way through the kitchen to the outside patio.

The concrete slabs had been washed clean and glistened in the sunshine with the new set of garden furniture placed where I can only assume Zoe had attacked Zach. It made my skin crawl to think we would be sitting close to where she had been struck by Alex. Ma was watching me closely and I smiled to reassure her that everything was okay.

"So, Alfie, how do you know my grandmother?" I asked with a friendly smile.

"Oh, Esther and I grew up together. We have been friends for longer than I care to imagine. She made the mistake of marrying the wrong guy, and I the wrong girl!" he guffawed before continuing, "But we were lucky in later life to find each other again. We have not been apart since."

"So you have been around since before I was born?" I asked curiously. My granddad had died a year before I was born and if he was correct, he was around during my childhood. How come I didn't remember him? Is that why I felt a familiar presence about him?

"Yes my dear!" he smiled. "Your grandmother used to place orders at my bakery for special meringues shaped like mice for her two gorgeous grand-daughters many years ago. Do you remember how much you liked those meringues? I never had the fortune of meeting you in person, though I knew of you through your grandma."

"Oh I see," I said feeling rather embarrassed at this man's intimate knowledge of my childhood's sweet tooth.

Suddenly a noise came from the kitchen and both Ma and Alfie turned to see who was coming. I thought it was Kumbi and quietly sipped my drink until I felt a pair of large hands on my shoulders, causing me to jump and spill my drink over the front of my sundress.

"Oh my, Mandy are you okay?" Ma trilled, jumping up to supply serviettes to mop the spillage. "Jason! You scared the poor girl," she said, scolding the big hands that still held my shoulders. I shivered, as the wetness seeped through to my thighs and turned my skin cold. I didn't want to admit that it was Jason's hands on me that caused my shiver more than anything else.

"Hi Bumblebee!" he said so close to my ear, invoking another involuntary shiver up my spine. I had to get a grip on myself. How could I react to this man in such a way? He was the father of my child and had apologised for his gross behaviour. I had kissed him and forgiven him in the hospital. He had saved me from a fire that could have killed Alex, Zachary and me! Maybe it was the lingering doubts that Alex had dredged up and my history with Jason who blew hot and cold at any given moment that caused the shivers.

I turned to smile directly at him, as he apologised for scaring me. Without removing his hands, he coaxed me out of the garden chair and back into the kitchen to clean

225

myself up. I caught Alfie and Ma smiling happily at me, as though this was all pre-planned. They hadn't known I was coming. I could only assume they were hoping we would find amicable ground again.

"I hope you've fully recovered from the fire," he said, gently caressing my back, as I focused my attention on cleaning my dress. The heat would take care of the rest, however it felt uncomfortable having a wet patch in front.

"Yes, yes I have," I replied, standing up straight and putting some distance between myself, and his roving hands. "I was hoping to see you today. I wanted to talk about us and a way forward."

His brown eyes brightened showing the little golden flecks deep inside. He took a step closer making me back up against the kitchen counter, whilst barring my escape with his body. A cold sweat broke out on my top lip and forehead, shivers wracked my body as his close proximity brought back memories of the rainy night when I told him he was the father of my son. My breath shortened. I had to get away before my knees buckled in fear.

"Why don't we join my grandma and her friend outside?" my voice stuttered, praying he would back off and set me free.

"I was actually just about to start work on my truck. How about joining me there, and we can talk more privately," he replied, turning slightly to see two pairs of eyes watching us through the kitchen window.

"Okay!" I jumped at the opportunity to get away.

We walked through the dim lounge and veranda out into the blinding sunlight and back under the cooler shade of the car port. The concrete floor was swept clean and only his tool box could be seen. It lay open with different sized spanners and screw drivers placed neatly in the divided sections. The bonnet of his car stood open like a gaping mouth of a monster.

"Were you here when I arrived Jason?" I asked, suddenly feeling unsure of my decision to follow him to the other side of the house.

"Yes I was. I didn't want to interrupt you and Ma since you haven't seen her since the hospital. I didn't think I needed to interfere in your reunion," he replied, stuffing his head into the gaping hole to check something that required half his body to disappear. He came out with a grease stain across his chest and his biceps flexed as he reached for a spanner and returned into the dark abyss.

"Thank you for that. It has been hard to face her after what happened to Zoe and us," I added, hoping to broach the subject gently. His body stiffened but he continued to fiddle with the engine.

"I came here to speak about my leaving the country again J!" I continued breathlessly, praying he wouldn't react badly. "I'm leaving the day after tomorrow. I'm taking Zach with me. We have completed our business here, and I need to get back to my job or else I'll be fired."

He slowly re-appeared from under the hood and stared blankly at me. I could see different emotions warring across his features and the hand clamped on the spanner scared me enough to step back against the metal burglar bars running along the side of the carport. They were hot and felt good and solid on my back, giving me a little strength to face the father of my child.

"What about us Bumblebee? Where do we stand?" he asked, turning and leaning his hip against the car, spanner still dangling from his right hand. "I thought we were going to try and be a family. Are you coming back?"

"Umm…yes I will come back. I need to figure out what sort of future we have together Jason," I lied. I could feel the temperature rising when he didn't hear what he

228

wanted, and I had to tamper it down somehow. "It has been such a rollercoaster ride since I've been back. I feel I need to return to where I have more control before I can move on. That's not to say that I don't see a future for us. I just need to end things on the other side of the ocean if that's okay," I continued, seeing the change on his face and a smile breaking out. Phew!

"Of course, I can understand that. And I can wait. I mean I waited this long didn't I?" he cackled, ducking back under the hood of the car as though everything was resolved.

"Jason, I have to ask you something without you getting upset." I braved stepping up to the car to lean in next to him. He seemed happy with my closeness and continued working, giving a grunt for me to continue.

"Why did you help my father all those years ago? I know the two of you didn't see eye to eye. I can't imagine he would come to you for money, so what happened?"

Jason turned to me from the darkness of the car's engine and grinned. "Your Dad would have swallowed his own tongue before asking me for money, even though he was in no position to refuse my help. The bank was foreclosing on his business because there were still questions about your involvement in the fire. He couldn't wait for the insurance to complete their investigation, with you gone, and things going from bad to worse with Zoe's injuries, he didn't have a choice. Ma approached me and asked me to step up and help the family. She knew that I was still in love with you, and Lola was a bitch. As soon as I knew that Lola had lied about the pregnancy to try to trap me into marriage, I dropped that whore like a tonne of bricks. No-one makes fun of me! No-one!" His deep voice resonated around the car port.

"So, you dropped Lola and helped my Dad out, becoming his partner and saving the business. Thank you Jason!"

"Ya! Ya!" he laughed to himself. "Those were the days. I had my own business to run, and I had to help your dad because he was so depressed. He didn't even come in to work most days. I only helped because I knew that you would have been there to help them Bumblebee. I did all this for you...for us. Now we have the company to ourselves. We will be set up nicely for all our kids together. Don't you see? If you hadn't run away, I would have found out you were pregnant sooner, and we could have been a family then. Your father would not have had a say in that either. You belong to me Mandy. You always did. Running away just made it sweeter to have you back. I'm not going to lose you again!" he smiled, eyes sparkling with happiness, as he reached to plant a wet kiss on my lips.

I smiled and took a step back. He grabbed me closer with his free hand and drew me to him. I could feel the hardness of his erection against my leg and his brown eyes darkened with unhinged passion, his thick brows fighting for dominance on his large forehead.

"Once wasn't enough for me Mands. The thought of you in that asshole's arms nearly drove me crazy. I knew you were sleeping with him. Otherwise, why would you have fought me when we went out? That was my mistake. I was so angry with you I thought you would like a taste of your own medicine with Zoe."

My eyes misted over at the memory, and I struggled to free myself from his grasp. He watched me like a cat with a mouse and held me tighter until I stopped struggling.

"My love I am so sorry I hurt you," he mumbled, pressing his lips against my forehead. I felt the heat from his skin and smelt the sticky sweat from his exertions. It was overpowering, and I had to get away. "You know I never meant to hurt you Mandy?" he said, shaking me a little in his grasp.

"Yes! Yes! I know that now," my voice squeaked, betraying my terror. I bit my lip to stop it from quivering. "Jason, I have to ask you this because it has been bugging me for a long time." I whispered.

"What is it?" he whispered back, using my soft voice as an excuse to lower his head closer to mine.

CHAPTER TWENTY-ONE

"Did you mess with my brakes because you were angry with me?" I asked. My heart beats drowned out all other sounds for a few milliseconds as I felt the heat rise from his tense body.

His change of mood blew up faster than an easterly breeze. "What if I did Mandy? What if I told you that I was angry, and your sister suggested that I teach you a little lesson? I want to be honest with you and it's torn me apart all this time!" he said, releasing me suddenly and turning back to the engine. He heard my gasp of surprise and glanced back, embarrassment and shame written all over his face.

"How could you Jason? You nearly killed our child! You were willing to risk that for what? Make Zoe happy? Show her what a mug you were that you could do her bidding? You hurt my baby, our baby, and you're just sorry?" Anger infused my bones and crushed any fear I had left in my system. "Did you start the fire at my house too? Did you set fire to my father's warehouse?" I shouted at his stiffening back.

He turned and swung the spanner at me, barely missing my face by an inch. I yelped and stumbled backwards, barely saving myself from tripping over his toolbox.

"You stupid ungrateful bitch! Of course, I didn't set fire to the warehouse, or your house. Yes I may have tampered with your brakes but nothing so serious that you wouldn't be able to stop. That must have been Zoe! She was with me and watched what I did. I would never have tried to hurt you. Don't you understand I love you?" he shouted, his chest rising and falling with anger.

"I've put up with your back-stabbing, ape-shit crazy family for years and never complained. Just waiting like a good little boy for you to return. I have put up with your crazy obsessive sister that will do anything to keep a hold on me. Yet, I stayed faithful to you. And when you decided to grace us with your presence, were you grateful? No, you come back with some guy I don't know, and a child you claim is mine. Of course, I was angry. I waited for you. I sacrificed my money and time looking after your stupid family so that you could come back to me. But what thanks do I get? You accusing me of hurting the same nut jobs I've been protecting all these years!"

He was fast and with his height and big arms, I barely managed to jump over the tool box before his large hands clamped down on me and dragged me back, my legs kicking and flailing like a ragdoll. I could feel the red anger raging inside, and I wanted to strike him. He didn't give me a chance. My arms were pinned at my sides, and my back pushed against the front of his open mouthed truck, its dark gaping hole waiting to swallow me!

"I know the truth about the fire at the warehouse Amanda. I know who started that fire and it wasn't me. It was your crazy grandmother! She thought she was helping your Dad by burning his fixed assets, so that the insurance would pay out, and he wouldn't be held liable to the contracts he couldn't fulfil. They had set the date, making sure no-one would be in the building. But you got that call and went off on your high horse, all because I had dumped you!"

"What?" I gasped, pushing at his thick forearms to support my aching back.

"Zoe is the one that called you. She was so angry with me, with you, and with Lola. She wanted to teach us all a lesson because she loved me. She knew what Ma was planning and thought she could get rid of you in the fire. I guess she didn't plan on getting caught in the smoke or that she would be burnt," he spat out.

"No! No!" I cried. "How could she? How could you?"

My legs buckled. Jason grabbed me to his chest and squeezed me tighter than an anaconda in a death grip.

"I'm sorry Bumblebee. I may be a villain in your eyes, even though you have been betrayed by those closest to you all this time. I had to keep all the secrets otherwise how could I show you that I protected your family all these years. They are like my own family…closer in fact."

"You knew all this time, and yet, you called me a liar Jason! You knew that I wasn't to blame for the fire. You and the rest of my family accused me of destroying everything. I have been holding on to my guilt all this time, not coming home because of the devastation I felt I was responsible for causing. You lied to me!" I sobbed, beating my hands hard against his barrel chest, trying to hurt him the way he hurt me. Pain seared through my injured shoulder but I didn't stop. The hurt inside outstripped the pain from torn tendons.

"Please Mandy, try to understand. You have to keep this to yourself too. You can't tell that friend of yours, or anyone else what happened. Otherwise, Esther will be sent to jail. She's too old and frail to survive such a punishment, and anyway, Alfred will never let that happen."

"What do you mean Alfred will never let that happen? What can he do to stop the truth from coming out?"

"Don't you remember him Mands? Didn't you recognise his face at all? Seriously? All this time you forgot about Alfie! Hahaha! No wonder you're confused. Alfred Beker is ..."

Thud!

Jason spasmed in my arms, his eyes confused and surprised. I screamed as blood trickled down the side of his head, just above his ear. Automatically my arms reached to catch his large shape as it fell sideways.

CRACK!

The sickening sound of his head connecting with the edge of the toolbox made my insides squelch in revulsion. His body jerked, red bubbles foaming from his open mouth and large brown eyes staring ahead at the wheels of the car. A dark pool of blood quietly slid down the side of the red toolbox and crept its way across the grey concrete floor towards my feet. My mouth worked in an O shape, silent screams trying to burst out. Warm amber eyes held mine, as my hands flapped uselessly as my sides, my brain short circuiting. Alfred smiled gently at me. He raised the crowbar, still dripping with bits of Jason's hair and blood.

"I'm sorry Amanda, Jason is right. We can't have you hurting your grandmother again, now can we? I've tried to do right by her, and you just keep on interfering, don't you?" he said in a calm sing-song voice. Without looking down, he stepped over Jason's inert body, moving gracefully towards me.

I darted to the left, running between Jason's truck and the black burglar bars fencing off the side of the car port. Dappled sunlight flicked like a camera lens, as I reached the end of the truck and ran across the jagged little stones towards my car. A sharp tug on my hair snapped me back, my legs flipping high into the air, as I fell heavily onto the shiny sharp edges of the stony driveway. My cry was swallowed up by the dry heat. I could feel my tears evaporating off my cheeks, as I lay in the blinding brightness of the midday sun, my eyes forced shut by the glare. A shadow blocked out the brightness. I opened my eyes to see the silhouette of Alfred standing over me, brandishing the crowbar above his head ready to strike.

"Alfie! No!" screamed Ma's voice from behind somewhere. "Don't hurt her! She's all I have now Alfie. Please!" The shrillness of her voice set my teeth on edge.

I gathered my strength and rolled away from him, scuttling on all fours and bruising my knees and palms on the stones in my desperate escape from this madman.

"Alfred, please let her go!" Ma cried, throwing her frail body onto him, as he tried to chase after me. I launched myself up into a run and managed to reach the car.

Where were my keys? Oh shit! They were left next to my drink at the back of the house.

I checked the windows. Yes! The driver's side had been left open because of the heat. Without wasting time I reached in, unlocked the door and jumped into the driver's seat, frantically winding up the window and locking the door. Alfred shook Ma off him and came round the car. Checking that all the doors were locked and searching the car was my next priority.

This was Alex's car, and I wasn't sure what he kept in it. Shaky fingers flicked open the cubby-hole and scratched around inside. I gripped a solid object and pulled it out. A cell phone! Oh God, please let it work I prayed. Alfred's voice muffled commands outside the window, demanding I come out of the car to talk. The loud tap, tap, tap, of the crowbar against my window made me drop the phone in fright. Shit! My hands were shaking so I couldn't even find the damn thing.

Suddenly the world exploded in glass. I screamed and covered my head, as glass flew in all directions over me. I could feel it cut into the skin on my arms and screamed again, trying to cower towards the passenger seat, away from the flying shards. Powerful hands reached in, clawing at my dress, as I pulled myself across the glass strewn seats, narrowly avoiding trapping my legs by the gearstick. My sweaty shaking fingers slipped off the knob to unlock the passenger door. Again, try again.

239

My hands slipped. Pressure on my hip and shoulder pulled them back towards the driver's side. My left hand reached out, clawing with nails and wet fingers. Pop! The door unlocked.

The hands holding my hip and shoulder gripped tight, pulling me back until I could feel his breath on my skin. I gripped the head rest of the passenger seat and launched my body forward, praying the door would open as I flew forward. My right hand connected with the handle in time to pull it back, unlocking the door. Momentum carried me out head first onto the shiny quartz waiting with jagged tips, as I fell. The shadow from the jacaranda tree moved sending long finger shadows across the stones, as I shot up dodging Ma's open arms. Alfred cursed and ran round the car as I cleared it, reaching for a grip on my wild hair streaming behind me. This time I ducked and scrambled forward, stumbling back up, as I ran to hide behind the bamboo bush on the left side of the driveway.

The heat beat down on my feverish head. My feet were on fire from twisting in the wedge shoes with thin shoe string straps. There was no time to check for injuries. Taking a deep breath I ran for freedom towards the front gate. The driveway felt long, and I could hear Alfred running behind me, followed by my grandmother's screams. My chest pounded and I prayed, oh I prayed so hard that Kumbi had not locked the gate again. If I reached that gate and it was locked, I would never see

Zachary again. Tears choked me. I tried to run faster in the killer wedges that felt so unstable, as the distance disappeared under my badly shoed feet. He was gaining on me ... this old man that had decided to protect my grandmother at all costs. How many people had he killed to protect her?

The black gate loomed before me. The chain and lock were hanging loose round the opening in the middle. It would be a matter of opening the gate and running. Come on Amanda, one more push! I tugged at the chain, watching it ripple, as it slid through the two loops. The lock caught just as he grabbed my shoulder. My hand reached back, and I pushed, as hard as I could, watching his wheezing body stumble backwards. My aching right arm shot forward to free the lock and I pushed the gate without looking back to see if he would follow. My body ran straight into strong arms that held me and trapped me in a warm embrace.

Relief flooded my body, choking my throat and making my knees buckle. Alex held me tight, his arms gently picking up my ragdoll body and helping me into an awaiting police car parked outside the gate. I looked around, surprised to see at least a dozen matching cars parked up on the pavement outside the house and grim faces watching me as they waited for their turn to enter the house of horror I had left behind.

"Are you alright?" Alex asked, gently touching me all over to check for broken bones or injuries and grimacing at the flecks of glass still stuck in my arms and hair.

"No, I'm okay," I said, giving him a shaky, teary smile. "I'm okay now."

He kissed me and hugged me to him, wrapping me up so tight I couldn't breathe. A tap at the window made him release me and look around to see a short man with a red bald head that seemed to absorb the sun turning it into a reflective beacon. He had a handkerchief in his hand and mopped his painful looking dome to remove some of the shine. Beady blue eyes looked at me, and I could feel an assessment on my health and stature just from his long hard stare.

"Is she okay Alex?" he asked, his deep voice resonating his gruff concern. "The grandmother is in custody and she is singing like a canary. Plus, thanks to your girlfriend here, we managed to find the link to your wife's death."

Alex sat up and released me from his grasp. "Can you stand up okay?" he asked, rubbing my cheek. I nodded and we both got out of the car to stand with this short man in his stripy green shirt and grey trousers.

"Hello again Detective Inspector Gallia," I greeted. He pumped my hand with enthusiasm and a brief smile before releasing it abruptly.

"Your grandmother's boyfriend is the one who set both the fires. He was asked by Esther Munford to help out her son who accumulated massive debt over the years preceding the warehouse fire. He came up with the idea of burning all the assets. The insurance company would have paid out any damages caused by an accidental mishap at the warehouse, and she assumed this would help your father pay off his debtors." Mr Gallia mopped his head again and looked across to see Alfred Beker being loaded into one of the police cruisers.

"From what we could pick up on the microphone you wore, the evidence you gathered proves your sister's involvement and her own vendetta against you. She decided to use the opportunity to get rid of you. Unfortunately, she was trapped by the fire. I can only assume that she screamed for help once she realised she couldn't escape. Sienna Edwards happened to be jogging in that direction and heard the cries for help. She tried to rescue your sister, never escaping the fire herself." He stopped to look at Alex who stared at me. I grabbed his hand and squeezed it and asked his inspector friend to continue.

"Mr Beker had been the Chief Inspector of the Harare Police Force for many years. He has friends high in government positions which made it easy to have Sienna Edward's body removed from the building before the investigators had a chance to find her. They had Zoe put into a mental hospital to recover and that is why you never found out she was hurt. They told no-one, not even your parents until the weekend she was supposed to return from her friend, Penelope's house. By then, her severe burns and lack of speech convinced your parents that you had started the fire. When the investigation was raised, it was Zoe's written testimony from the hospital that held you responsible. A witness who saw you leave the warehouse put the blame squarely on your shoulders.'

'After arranging for a Jane Doe hit and run case close to Sienna's Edwards listed residence they were able to cover up her death. After that it was a matter of containing the damages of your involvement in the fire to vindicate you and release the money. With your disappearance to the UK, they could not complete the investigation and the insurance company refused to pay out to your parents. Your friend Jason stepped up with the financing at your grandmother's request. When you returned, it seems that things escalated between your sister and you. We found fingerprints on your car matching Jason's and Zoe's and accelerants at the house that belonged Alfred Beker's bakery."

"Did my parents know the truth?" I asked.

David shook his beaconed dome. "No, as far as we can tell, they honestly thought you had started the fire and believed Zoe. They assumed it was a mistake all along."

"We thought Jason had started the fires out of anger or hatred!" I cried, my tears falling at the thought of how brutally he had died.

Alex replied, "No. I think Jason had genuinely loved you to the point of obsession. I don't think he realised how well matched he and Zoe were in their obsessions. He probably had come to the house to reconcile himself with you and found it on fire, as he admitted. He helped me get you and Zach out before we were engulfed in the flames. I wasn't strong enough to push you through the window." He sighed admitting the events. I drew closer to him, hoping he knew that I still considered him my hero.

"You came close to being killed there Ms Glenson," came the surprising comment from David Gallia. "Mr Beker had snuck into the house, knocking you out, locking your door so that no-one could rescue you once the fire caught on. Thanks to Alex here, he managed to save you and your son at the risk of his own life!" David continued. I smiled and gave Alex a hug, rubbing my tear-stained face against his clean smelling shirt. My heart and head pounded at the same time with all the pieces of the jigsaw puzzle of my life falling into place.

"What will happen to my grandmother?" I asked, spotting her small face at the back of the black and white police car.

"Based on her involvement in the crimes, she might do time for perpetrating the warehouse fire and knowingly withholding information on the death of Sienna Edwards and the injuries sustained by her granddaughter Zoe. But with her age and her sickness, I think the courts might be lenient."

I sighed and closed my eyes. Ma was the most loving person I remembered from my childhood and it broke my heart to think she was involved. The men talked over my head as I swooned to a place that blotted out all the hurt and pain, trying to grapple with the truth at last. I opened my eyes in time to see the police cruisers pull away with Ma sitting in the back, a soft smile on her face as she looked at me whilst the car drove past.

Alex hugged me to his chest and dropped a kiss on my forehead. He said, "Let's go home!"

CHAPTER TWENTY-TWO

Wind chimes clanged together and their soft music sent a mesmerising tune into the cold wet night. Christmas lights twinkled in the window. A Christmas tree shone with bright red and gold decorations, a star flickering incandescently at the top. Presents were crammed under its soft branches and a toy railway track surrounded its base. Dean Martin's charming voice crooned over the radio, as the smell of gingerbread and cinnamon filled the air. Zachary sat watching his favourite television show and nibbled on a gingerbread man that he had decorated earlier with his mother. Amanda busied herself tidying up the sitting room and entrance way for the hundredth time, stopping to check her hair and dress in the hallway mirror.

The doorbell made her jump and she straightened her already pristine dress. Zachary ran past her to the front door and before she could shout at him to stop, he pulled the door open to let in the cold wind and a tall shadowy figure wiping his feet on the door mat.

"Hey buddy! Merry Christmas!" Alex grinned as Zachary jumped into his arms and gave him an enormous gingerbread hug.

Amanda stepped forward to help close the door on her two favourite men and reached up to receive her own kiss that thrilled her to her toes. After removing his damp overcoat, gloves and scarf Alex followed Amanda and Zachary into the warm toasty living room. A fire burned low in the grate and the children's programme rattled off in the background with Dean Martin competing on the radio. The smell of homemade gingerbread made his tummy rumble.

"I hope you don't mind, that I brought a few more presents for my favourite people," he smiled, creases showing on the sides of his mouth and his dark eyes twinkling.

"Alex, thank you, you shouldn't have worried," Amanda said, smiling and reaching to hug his arm. He wrapped his arms about her, letting Zachary offload the presents under the tree whilst he kissed her fully and hugged her to him, his aftershave wrapping her in its woody masculine scent.

"I love you so much," she whispered against his jacket and he tightened his grasp.

Kissing her again, he whispered into her hair, "I love you too!" He turned to watch an excited little boy pull out the last present from the bag. "Oh Zachary, that's a special one for your mum," he said holding out his hand for the velvet box. Zachary and Alex shared a conspiratorial grin.

"What is it?" Amanda asked, excitement changing her eyes to a soft hazel green.

"Open it," Alex and Zachary both said in unison and laughed. Alex reached over and pulled Zachary into his warm embrace. They stood in front of Amanda, both grinning like mischievous schoolboys waiting for a prank to succeed as they waited excitedly for her to open the blue velvet box. Amanda's hands shook as she gently opened the box. She gasped at the beautiful ring sitting inside, twinkling with little diamonds clustered round a gorgeous sapphire. Her eyes filled with tears of joy. She looked up to see Alex and Zachary slowly going down on bended knee in front of her.

"Amanda Glenson, would you honour me by becoming my wife and staying by my side until the day I die?" Alex asked, happiness and fear mixed in his dark eyes.

Amanda took a moment to look at the beautiful man in front of her who had the unflinching love of her son and who made her feel safe, warm and loved and nodded with her heart fit to burst. She couldn't think of being anywhere else than by his side, for the rest of her life. At last, she had a family she could call her own. She sank to her knees and hugged her son and her future husband.

The wind chimes rattled under the brisk breeze and a shadow fell across the window overlooking the garden. Hazel green eyes sparkled in the darkness and a twisted grin glittered, as the clouds passed and the moon appeared. Zoe watched with interest at the happy family moment and sighed. Wasn't it her turn for happiness?

She grinned, a beautiful grotesque smile pulled down on one side. "I guess I had better take what's mine!"

Dear Reader,

I hope you enjoyed Deception.

Please check out my other books available from Amazon at:

http://www.amazon.co.uk/s/ref=nb_sb_noss/279-6455384-2733132?url=search-alias%3Daps&field-keywords=eloise+de+sousa

or, if you would like to go straight to my publishing site, please click on:

www.lulu.com/spotlight/eloisedesousa

For further updates on my current books and work-in-progress, follow my blog at:

http://eloisedesousa.wordpress.com

Your support is greatly appreciated.

Thank You.

Eloise

#0062 - 300316 - C0 - 210/143/14 - PB - DID1407486